THE PHILOSOPHY AND PRACTICE
OF POLARITY MAGIC

THE PHILOSOPHY
AND PRACTICE
OF POLARITY MAGIC
A Secret Wisdom of Sex

John Michael Greer

AEON

First published in 2024 by
Aeon Books

British Library Cataloguing in Publication Data

A C.I.P. for this book is available from the British Library

ISBN-13: 978-1-80152-148-2

Typeset by Medlar Publishing Solutions Pvt Ltd, India

www.aeonbooks.co.uk

CONTENTS

CHAPTER 1

The nature of polarity magic

There are many different kinds of magic. This book is about one of them. There are also many ways in which polarity can be used in magic. This book, again, is about one of them. To make sense of what is to follow, it may be helpful to begin by talking a little about what these two words "magic" and "polarity" mean. By doing so I will start the process of explaining what kind of magic and what kind of polarity this book is intended to teach you to learn, practice, and put to work in your life.

Dion Fortune, the most important figure in the development of modern polarity magic, defined magic as "the art and science of causing changes in consciousness in accordance with will." That definition is considerably trickier than many people realize. Notice that it doesn't define whose consciousness is being changed, or whose will directs the process! That very ambiguity reflects the essential nature of magic, for any center of consciousness and any act of will can play a part in a magical working.

According to the teachings of occult philosophy, consciousness is not limited to the inside of certain lumps of meat called human brains. It is present in all things to a greater or lesser degree, including those things most people consider "inanimate." The mage (the practitioner of magic) who learns how to do so, and pursues the necessary practices with the necessary dedication, can commune with the intelligences present in all things seen and unseen, and thus cause changes in their consciousness as well as his or her own.

According to occult philosophy, equally, will is just as pervasive in the cosmos as consciousness. It is the force behind all existence, the power that drives the entire universe, and it is present in all things to a greater or lesser degree. The mage can learn to sense the movements of will in the cosmos: this is the basis of divination. The mage can also learn to balance and direct some of these movements: this is the basis of magic properly so called.

There are many different schools, styles, and traditions of magic. Among the most widely practiced varieties of magic in the industrial societies of the modern West these days are folk magic, Neopagan magic, and ceremonial magic. Folk magic is a convenient term for the diverse collections of magical lore handed down in folk cultures around the world, especially but not only in rural areas and ethnic communities. Neopagan magic is an equally useful label for the magical practices used by participants in Neopaganism, a new religious movement that emerged in the twentieth century; most people these days are familiar with the most popular variety of Neopaganism, the religion of Wicca.

Ceremonial magic is a name for a body of formal magical teachings that until recently were practiced in occult lodges. These teachings descended in literate Western culture from the occult traditions of the Renaissance, and ultimately came from the rich magical traditions of the ancient world. The material in this book comes from the traditions of ceremonial magic, and from a particular school of ceremonial magic at that. To avoid confusion, readers may find it useful to keep this in mind as we proceed.

The primary tools of ceremonial magic are will and imagination. All the implements of the operative ceremonial mage—the wands, swords, cups, and pentacles, the robes and altar cloths of many colors, the flickering candles and billowing incense—are simply devices to strengthen and focus the imagination and direct it in response to the mage's will. Ritual is an implement of the same kind. Ritual may be defined as symbolic action. Any act becomes a ritual if it is used to represent something beyond itself, and it becomes a magical ritual if that representation becomes a pattern through which will and imagination shape the subtle substance that is the raw material of magic.

This last factor, the subtle substance magic works with, is the element of magic that takes it outside the realm of psychology and into worlds where today's conventional materialist thinking cannot follow. Modern Western industrial societies are unique in human history for refusing to admit the existence of something that has been an ordinary element of human existence in every other culture and age: the life force, a subtle influence connected with biological life, which can be shaped and directed in certain ways by the human mind.

Most languages around the world and throughout the ages include words for it. It is *qi* in Chinese, *ki* in Japanese and Korean, *prana* in Sanskrit and many other languages of the Indian subcontinent, *mana* in the Polynesian languages, *ruach* in Biblical Hebrew, *pneuma* in ancient Greek, and so on through the litany of the world's ways of human speech. Until the time of the scientific revolution, the same concept was just as common in Europe as it was elsewhere. The Latin word *spiritus*, the root of the English word "spirit," was the standard term for it in educated circles. It also had its own vernacular names in every living European language.

For complex cultural reasons, however, the thinkers who spearheaded the scientific revolution embraced a dogmatic materialist ideology that denied the existence of the life force. That same ideology has been fixed in place in Western cultures ever since. It is defended by influential political and economic interests and reinforced by potent emotional commitments. To this day, you can reduce distinguished scientists to spluttering rage by suggesting that the life force is a reality. Try it and see!

Be this as it may, there has always been a lively minority of thinkers and practitioners in the Western world who refused to accept the abolition of so basic an element of human experience as the life force. Ceremonial mages have very often belonged to this minority, not least because the life force is the medium through which magic functions. Different schools of magic have given the life force various names. The term for the life force that is used in this book is the one that has been standard in occult circles for the last century and a half: the ether.[1]

The nature and functions of the ether will be discussed in detail in the chapters that follow. For now, two points are crucial. The first point

---

[1] This is not the same as the chemical called "ether," better known as nitrous oxide. A complex history lies behind the shared name.

is that the ether is among other things the force behind human sexuality and life itself: "the force that through the green fuse drives the flower," in Dylan Thomas's evocative phrase. The flow of energy that many people sense in sexual arousal is a movement of the ether, and like any other expression of the etheric realm, it responds to will and imagination if these are skillfully handled. The second is that in sex, as in all its manifestations, the ether has two equal and opposite manifestations: that is to say, it is subject to polarity.

What is polarity? We can define it as the tendency for all phenomena to take the form of two equal and opposite forces. In his 1913 textbook of occult philosophy *The Kybalion*, the influential American occultist William Walker Atkinson summed up polarity neatly as one of seven basic principles of the cosmos. His definition is worth citing in full: "Everything is dual; everything has poles; everything has its pair of opposites; like and unlike are the same; opposites are identical in nature, but different in degree; extremes meet; all truths are but half-truths; all paradoxes may be reconciled."[2]

Polarity is thus found in all things and expresses itself in many different ways. Many of these have a significant role in the symbolism used in magical practice. Among mages who practice traditional Western ceremonial magic, by contrast, the phrase "polarity magic" means something much more specific: a specific system of magical practice, performed by two or more people together, that works with the astral light by redirecting and sublimating the influences and energies of sex.

Polarity magic has roots going back to antiquity, and certain forms of it were practiced in the Middle Ages and the Renaissance. In its present form, however, it began to take shape in the nineteenth century as Western ceremonial mages encountered the extraordinarily rich magical and spiritual traditions of Asia, and began to envision their own traditions in new ways as a result. Out of the resulting ferment came the work of Dion Fortune, who created the first thoroughly developed modern system of polarity magic. Her students, and more recent mages working along the same lines, have built extensively on the foundations she set down, while revising some of her less helpful ideas.

Are there other forms of polarity that can be useful in magic? Of course, and if you prefer to work with these other forms there is no

---

[2] Atkinson 1913, p. 10.

reason why you should avoid doing so. Are there other ways to use erotic energies in magic? Of course, and if you prefer one or more of these other ways, here too the door is open. Now and again certain authors of books on magic have treated one kind or another of method for working with erotic energies as the be-all and end-all of magic, and implied or outright stated that anyone who fails to make use of sexual polarity in their magical work has fallen short of some standard or other. This is nonsense. In magic, as in the rest of human life, there's no such thing as a single right way for everybody.

With this in mind, it may be worth making an explicit point here. *In the pages that follow, the phrase "polarity magic" will be used to refer to a specific approach to magical working that functions through the sublimation of erotic energies between two or more people.* That is what this book is about, and it's all that this book is about. Many other things can be called "polarity magic," but they will not be discussed in this book. There are other books on those subjects, and readers who are interested in such things can find them easily enough. This point may seem obvious, given what's already been discussed in this chapter, but misunderstandings about the subject of this book are so common these days that a little extra clarity is worthwhile.

The kind of polarity magic this book discusses is a powerful, effective, and balanced way of working magic. It is not to everyone's taste, nor is it something that everyone can or should do, but then neither is anything else. It is a mode of ceremonial magic, and it can be learned and practiced within every system of ceremonial magic I know of, with good results.

These days, however, anything and everything that has to do with human sexuality has become a battleground in the perennial squabbles between competing factions in the ongoing culture wars of our society. For this reason among others, several additional points should be made clear before we proceed any further.

Polarity is not identity

Those of my readers who haven't been hiding under a rock for the last decade or two will be well aware that gender identity is a hot-button issue these days. On one end of the dispute are those people who insist that a person's gender identity ought to be defined strictly by their biological sex. On the other end are those people who insist just as loudly that a person's gender identity is whatever they feel it is. The resulting shouting match produces, as usual, considerably more heat than light. Some books and other resources on polarity magic have taken up explicit positions on one side or the other, and nearly all have been drawn into the fray.

This book will not do the same, because the kind of polarity discussed in the pages that follow—sexual polarity—is unrelated to personal gender identity. You can see this clearly enough in the most material form of sexual polarity working, the kind that results in pregnancy and childbirth. To father a child, a person must have testes that produce viable sperm. To bear a child, a person must have a uterus that can carry the child to term. The personal gender identity of the people in question may determine whether they want to have a child but it does not determine whether they are capable of doing so. That depends on biology, not identity.

A central teaching of traditional occultism holds that the material world we experience with the five ordinary senses is one of several different planes of being. Another core teaching holds that human beings have bodies on more than one of these planes. (All this will be discussed in detail later on in this book.) These other bodies, like your material body, are objective realities, though only the material body is biological. Just as your ability to father or bear a child depends on certain arrangements of your material body, your ability to do certain other things depends on certain arrangements of other bodies.

Polarity magic of the kind taught in this book is one of these things. Certain arrangements of the etheric and astral bodies, to drop briefly into occult jargon, are necessary in order to fill certain roles in polarity magic. Like the arrangements of the material body that make fathering or bearing a child possible, those arrangements are not defined by a person's sense of their own gender identity. In some cases, though by no means all, they can be identified from the conformation of the person's material body and from the nature of that person's sexual desires. All this will be covered in detail as we proceed.

This book passes no judgment concerning anyone's sense of their own identity. It does not address issues of personal identity at all. Gender identity is irrelevant to polarity magic, because the forces that move through polarity magic are transpersonal, and indeed impersonal. It is therefore essential for readers to realize that this book is about sexual polarity, not about gender identity. As a result, certain common words are used in this book purely in a sexual sense, and should not be taken as statements concerning gender identity.

In the pages that follow, accordingly, words such as "man" and "male" will refer to adult human beings who were born with penises, testicles, and XY or XYY sex chromosomes. Words such as "woman" and "female" will refer to adult human beings who were born with vaginas, uteruses, ovaries, and XX or XXX sex chromosomes. Words such as "intersex" will be used for the small minority of people (less than 2% of the adult population) who do not fit into either of the two categories just listed. Our language doesn't contain words for biological sex distinct from the terms for gender identity, so these will have to do.

One other issue of identity needs to be mentioned here. Since polarity working depends on sexual and emotional attraction, issues of sexual orientation can't be avoided when discussing polarity work. Here, too, polarity is not identity. It's tolerably common these days to meet people who identify as straight but have same-sex erotic relationships, and people who identify as gay or lesbian but have erotic relationships with people of the opposite sex.

When this book uses words such as "straight" and "heterosexual," accordingly, it means erotic attraction between biological males and biological females, irrespective of the orientation with which the participants identify. When it uses words such as "gay" or "lesbian," it refers to erotic attraction between members of the same sex, irrespective of the participants' sense of their own orientations. When it uses words such as "bisexual," it refers to those individuals of either sex who are attracted erotically to members of both sexes. Awkward as this may be in today's overheated rhetorical environment, effective polarity magic depends on precision in these matters.

Polarity magic is not sex magic

The interface between sexuality and occultism gets plenty of attention in the venues where occultism and popular culture rub elbows. Nearly all of that attention, however, focuses on sexual intercourse in a ritualized setting. This isn't just an effect of the mass media, though the notion that occultism is mostly about hot sex in strange outfits has been a theme for lurid media stories since the days when the media consisted of broadsheets hot from the letterpress. As we'll discuss in a later chapter, sexual intercourse as a ritual act has been part of certain traditions of occultism in the Western world for a very long time, and the same thing can be traced back in Asian countries for much longer.

That is not what this book is about, however. The polarity workings explored here are not sex magic in that sense; that is to say, they do not include sexual intercourse. The energies that drive these workings are erotic in nature, but the work does not involve sexual contact of any kind. Quite the contrary, if a polarity working results in sexual activity, the working fails, and not in any abstract way. The energy that would have gone into making magic grounds out instead in the sex act, leaving the working ineffectual.

The basic principle of polarity magic is the sublimation of sexual energy. "Sublimation" here is a technical term borrowed from the language of alchemy. To sublimate any force is to raise it from one plane to a higher plane. The movements of the ether that most people experience as sexual and emotional attraction, given free rein, will do their best to follow their natural course down all the way into the material plane, resulting in sex and (biology permitting) childbirth. Those same movements can be redirected to less material planes, and when this is done, the results can be magical in every sense of the word.

Given common attitudes toward sexuality in today's industrial nations, it's not surprising that many people assume that there must be something wrong with sublimating sexual energy—that any such process must be rooted in hatred or fear of sexuality, for example, or that sublimation is somehow sick or wrong. Common as such notions are these days, they're mistaken, and betray a complete misunderstanding of what's being discussed. Polarity working does not require anyone to give up sex entirely, so they can sublimate all their sexual energy into magical work. In fact, most mages I know of who practice polarity workings are married, or have some other outlet for an ordinary sex life. Polarity work requires only that the primary participants in the working sublimate the sexual and emotional attraction they feel toward one and only one person—the person with whom they are doing polarity work.

Most of us have plenty of experience with setting aside sexual or romantic feelings toward another person, when for some reason or other it is inappropriate to express or act on such feelings. Polarity work differs from that common human experience in two ways. The first is that everyone involved in a polarity working knows in advance what to expect, so no one ends up embarrassed or humiliated by having their feelings rebuffed. The second is that the feelings in question don't just hang around, leaving one or more people in a state of frustration. The whole point of polarity working is that the sexual energies present in the working are sublimated, redirected, and set flowing in new channels in order to accomplish magic.

When polarity magic is done successfully, in fact, the participants end up feeling a sense of satisfaction that in many cases resembles nothing so much as the afterglow from sexual intercourse. Here's how polarity mage Christine Campbell Thompson described it in the less explicit language of an earlier era: "When we got back I felt completely different: my voice was warm and vibrating, and I had that sense of complete fulfillment that comes to women in certain circumstances."[3] It takes patience, skill, and a certain amount of practice to achieve such states reliably—but this is equally true of ordinary lovemaking, of course. On the other hand, if a ritual of polarity magic consistently fails to provide this kind of satisfaction, and leaves the participants in a state of frustrated arousal instead, it's a safe assumption that serious mistakes are being made in the work.

And if this kind of working doesn't interest you? That's fine. Again, polarity magic is only one of many ways to work with erotic energies in a magical or spiritual context, and erotic energies are only one of many potential sources of power for magical work. As already noted, some incautious writers have claimed from time to time that this or that kind of magical working is the supreme secret of magic, and polarity magic has come in for this kind of overenthusiastic praise now and again in occult literature. The fact of the matter is that no one kind of magical working is the be-all and end-all of magic. The reason for this is simple: people differ, and the magical methods that work best for them therefore differ just as widely.

Polarity magic therefore works very well for some people, moderately well for many people, and poorly or not at all for others. It cannot and should not be for everyone—and this means among other things that its practitioners generally must set strict limits on who can and cannot take part in any given sequence of polarity workings.

_____

[3] Quoted in Richardson and Hughes 1992, p. 53. "Got back" refers to her return from a visionary experience—one of the magical states of consciousness that can be achieved through polarity workings.

Polarity magic is not inclusive

This point is challenging for many people nowadays to grasp, and so it's best approached through a metaphor. Imagine for a moment that four musicians are in the habit of getting together once a week to play Baroque string quartets. All four of them have spent years learning how to play their instruments so they can handle even the most technically difficult pieces by Bach, Telemann, Mozart, and other Baroque masters, and they put in the daily musical practice necessary to maintain and develop their skills.

One day, just as they are getting ready to launch into a Bach quartet, a loud knocking sounds on the door of their practice space. One of the violinists sets down her instrument and goes to see who it is. When she opens the door, in come a dozen people with ukeleles, saying, "Hi! We heard about your group and we want to play with you."

It turns out that half of them have never played a ukelele before and the other half have very modest amounts of experience, ranging from a few weeks to a few years of very occasional playing. None of them can read music, and none of them are willing to learn how. Nor do they have the least interest in Baroque music. What they want to do is strum their ukeleles and sing "Tiny Bubbles." When the Baroque musicians suggest anything else, the ukelele players get defensive and insist that "Tiny Bubbles" is a perfectly good tune. When the Baroque musicians finally give up, pack up their instruments, and head for the door, they are followed by angry shouts of "Bigots!"

This is a fictional account, but it serves to introduce a painfully common experience. No, as far as I know, classical musicians don't have to put up with this sort of thing, but ceremonial magicians certainly do, and so do other groups in the alternative-spirituality scene who are trying to do something beyond the lowest common denominator of magical or spiritual practice. This is one of the main reasons why so many serious magical lodges and other groups working ceremonial magic keep a low public profile, and accept new members only by personal recommendation followed by an extended course of solitary study. That, too, gets its share of angry denunciations these days.

The ideology behind the fictional ukelele players in my metaphor, and their all too real equivalents in the magical scene, can be described as *coercive inclusivism*. It's the belief that nobody can be permitted to do something unless everybody gets to participate. Central to coercive inclusivism is the false claim that the only reason anyone is ever excluded from anything is bigotry on the part of the excluders. Are some people excluded from some things due to bigotry? Of course, but there are other reasons for exclusion—some of them very good ones.

People who haven't graduated from medical school and passed their board exams as surgeons, for example, are excluded from performing brain surgery. People who aren't qualified structural engineers are excluded from designing bridges. In the industrial world today, at least, people of every gender and ethnicity who want to become brain surgeons or structural engineers have a good chance of doing so, if they're willing to work hard and earn the necessary grades. People who aren't willing to put in the work aren't allowed to do these things because they don't have the knowledge, experience, and competence to do it without killing people.

For a less drastic example, let's return to the earlier metaphor and assume for a moment that you don't know how to play a musical instrument and have never learned to read music. Unless you're willing to put in the time and effort to learn these things, you are excluded from playing Bach. No law prevents you from doing so, nor is that exclusion a matter of bigotry. You're perfectly free to go to the nearest music store, buy a violin and some Bach sheet music, and give it your best try, but you won't be able to produce the notes Bach had in mind. If you take your new violin and the sheet music to a local symphony orchestra and insist that you ought to be allowed to play with them, you won't get far, either—not because the symphony members are bigots, but because their job is to play classical music and you don't know how to do that.

Ceremonial magic is much like classical music. A beginner needs years of instruction, study, and practical experience to learn how to do it competently, and a disciplined commitment to daily practice is as important to the ceremonial magician as it is to the concert violinist. If you haven't done the necessary training and aren't willing to commit to the daily practice, you can't do the things with your consciousness, thoughts, and vital energies that ceremonial magicians have to do in order for their magic to accomplish what it's supposed to accomplish. It really is as simple as that.

Are there kinds of magic that don't require that kind of training and discipline? Of course. Many forms of folk magic and Neopagan magic can be practiced successfully by people with little or no magical experience. Are people who want to do these other kinds of magic justified in getting together to practice it? Of course. In terms of my metaphor, there certainly ought to be opportunities for people to get together to strum ukeleles and enjoy themselves singing "Tiny Bubbles," or whatever else they want to sing. There also ought to be opportunities for ukelele players to get together with classical musicians and see what kind of common ground they can find between their different styles of music, provided that all parties are interested in this kind of exploration. Yet there should also be opportunities available for people who simply want to play Bach, Mozart, and Telemann.

All ceremonial magic is exclusive, in the same way that playing Bach's music is exclusive: you need certain skills to do it, and if you don't have those skills and aren't willing to put in the hard work needed to develop them, you'll be forever on the outside looking in. Learning how to acquire the skills in question is easier now than it has ever been. There are literally hundreds of books that provide detailed instruction in the practice of ceremonial magic for complete beginners; half a dozen of my books are among them. You can pick up one of those books and learn how it's done by simply following the instructions in the book and putting in the daily practice. (That's how I originally learned magic, for instance.) Yet polarity magic has another level of exclusivity, which also needs to be understood before we can proceed.

The power behind polarity magic is the movement of the ether that most people experience as erotic and emotional attraction. If two people are to perform a polarity working, they both need to have the necessary magical skills, but they also need to feel erotic and emotional attraction toward each other, and they need to be willing to put those feelings into magical work, rather than expressing them in any more ordinary way. Those requirements aren't negotiable. Trying to perform a polarity working without mutual erotic and emotional attraction is like filling the gas tank of your car with tap water, and then setting out on a long road trip.

What makes this challenging is that erotic and emotional attraction are not subject to ideology. They can't be forced, and they can't be faked. They're present or they're not, and if they're not, except in certain equally narrow conditions that will be discussed later, the two people in question can't work polarity magic together.

A person who doesn't feel erotic or emotional attraction thus can't work polarity magic at all. A person who is uncomfortable with sexual or emotional attraction is probably better off avoiding any involvement with polarity magic. Two people who don't feel erotic or emotional attraction to each other, while they might be able to do polarity work with other people, can't make it work between themselves. That doesn't make such people inferior or inadequate. It simply means that this particular mode of magical practice, in this situation, isn't something they can or should do together, or at all. Again, there are many other branches of magical practice, some of them just as demanding and powerful as polarity magic, and they can pursue those and get as much success as their efforts earn them.

In today's world, however, that simple reality is unacceptable to various groups of people. It's an interesting inversion of the ideas of an earlier age. Puritanically minded people back in Victorian times insisted that people shouldn't have sexual or romantic feelings toward certain other people, and got furious when those feelings popped up anyway. By contrast, their opposite numbers these days insist that people ought to have sexual or romantic feelings toward certain other people, and get just as furious when the feelings don't show up on demand. Silly? Of course it is, but it's astonishing how many people have never noticed that the opposite of one bad idea is usually another bad idea.

This doesn't mean that the prejudices of an earlier day, or those of specific writers (very much including Dion Fortune), ought to be enforced on polarity workings. It means that those who choose to pursue polarity work have the right and the duty to decide for themselves who they want to work with in this very intimate and emotionally vulnerable mode of magical practice. It also means that nobody else has any right, or any business, demanding that polarity workers make such choices in terms of an arbitrary ideology. That's equally true whether the ideology in question is conservative, liberal, or something else.

The wind of the Spirit bloweth where it listeth, as the Bible says. In the same way, though on a very different plane, the currents of desire and attraction flow where they choose, not where we choose. The transpersonal and indeed impersonal nature of the forces that govern polarity magic can be seen clearly in this fact.

With these points firmly in mind, we can proceed. In many magical traditions, knowing how something came into being is crucial for understanding its nature and its powers, and so we will begin with a brief history of polarity magic.

CHAPTER 2

A history of polarity magic

E ven in ancient Athens, at the zenith of Greece's cultural flowering, drinking parties varied in their intellectual content. Some were nothing more than excuses to get roaring drunk while cuddling up to one's lover or making passes at the scantily clad flute players who provided musical entertainment. Others featured conversations at all levels from the latest gossip from the marketplace to the latest trends in philosophy and the arts. Few if any of them, however, could have featured the extraordinary intellectual richness of the party that Plato invented as the scene of one of his greatest dialogues, the *Symposium*, to frame a discussion of the philosophy of love.

Plato's real name was Aristocles; he got the nickname everyone remembers because of his very broad shoulders. He was born in 427 BC, when Athens was still the most important city in Greece, and died in 347 BC in a defeated city impoverished by war, revolution, and pandemic disease. Over the course of a long and busy life as a philosopher, writer, and teacher, he made an enduring imprint on the thought of the Western world. Alfred North Whitehead, himself no slouch as a philosopher, was not exaggerating when he suggested that all of Western philosophy could be called a collection of footnotes to Plato.

Philosophers did not yet specialize in Plato's time. Each of his many dialogues thus took a different subject—politics, physics, linguistics, and the list goes on—and explored the subject by having an assortment of speakers with interesting ideas have an impromptu debate on it. Socrates, who was Plato's teacher until he was executed by the Athenian government in 399 BC, plays a central role in many of the dialogues, including the *Symposium*. Many of the other leading intellectual and cultural figures who were part of the life of Athens during Socrates' time also appear in the pages of Plato's dialogues.

Most of the viewpoints explored in the *Symposium* have no direct bearing on the theme of this book and can be left for readers to discover for themselves. The section of the dialogue that matters for our present purposes is the speech by Socrates that forms the culmination of the book's argument. The guests at the drinking party have been talking about the nature of love, presenting different narratives about its nature. Urged by the others to make his own contribution to the discussion, Socrates tells the others of his conversations with Diotima of Mantinea, a prophetess and wise woman who instructed him on the subject.

The central theme of the teaching she passed on to Socrates was the education of desire. All human desire, she said, aims for the beautiful, the true, and the good, but attempts to find these in a dizzying range of objects and experiences, with very mixed success. The wise, recognizing this, learn how to move from a desire for one particular person's beautiful body to a desire for beautiful things in general, then to a desire for beauty in less material forms, and eventually to the quest to contemplate beauty as it exists in the spiritual realm, where it is among the Ideas or Forms, the true realities of which the material world is a cheap imitation.

Diotima's teachings, reframed by Plato in some of the finest Greek prose ever written, went on to become one of the primary sources of the entire tradition of Western mysticism. Reworked in later centuries by Christian theologians, who inserted their god in place of Plato's impersonal Ideas, it gave rise to a way of thinking about the spiritual quest that became all but universal throughout the diverse Christian tradition. When you hear preachers talk about loving God as the way to salvation, and of moving from earthly loves to heavenly love, that's Diotima's voice you hear whispering through their words.

Yet the same concept, applied in a less narrowly theological sense, murmured through the crawlspaces of the Western mind in many other ways over the centuries that followed. The tradition of courtly love in the Middle Ages is a case in point. Most people these days still remember dimly that in the heyday of chivalry, each knight was expected to cultivate a romantic attachment to a lady and do noble deeds in her name. J.R.R. Tolkien, who cultivated a lifelong taste for bawdy humor, used to enjoy repeating the words of an Oxford undergraduate who unthinkingly referred to courtly love as "a vast medieval erection." The undergraduate was right, of course—there is a strong sexual element to the entire tradition of courtly love—but there was more going on among those knights and ladies than ordinary sexual craving.

The traditions of courtly love emerged in the south of France in the eleventh century. That place and time saw an extraordinary flowering of culture and magic, setting currents in motion that remain vibrant today. While Eleanor of Aquitaine, Marie of Provence, and their sister aristocrats were holding "Courts of Love" to rule on whether this or that knight had behaved in a suitably romantic fashion, they and their courtiers were listening eagerly to tales of adventure, newly brought from Wales and Brittany, about a king named Arthur and a mysterious object called the Grail. Meanwhile, in the same part of France, circles of Gnostic teachers and students were launching the Albigensian heresy, and Rabbi Isaac the Blind of Toulouse was creating the first draft of the traditions that became the Cabala.

Courtly love drew from the same cultural context. In theory, and sometimes in practice, those who followed the tradition pursued the same approach to the education of desire that Socrates learned from Diotima, refining ordinary erotic attraction into strength of character and a commitment to high ideals. Since these customs ended up becoming enshrined in some of the most popular literature of the age, and were passed down through the generations thereafter in that form, some knowledge of the power of sublimated erotic energy stayed current all through the Western world in the centuries that followed.

That knowledge strayed more than once into the practice of magic. In the magical writings of Giordano Bruno, who was burned at the stake for heresy in 1600, erotic energy is a central theme, directed by the mage to shape consciousness.[4] A few other writers on magic in the Renaissance and the early modern period followed Bruno's lead in one way or another. The Renaissance flowering of magic generated a violent

---

[4] Culianu 1987 is a classic study of Bruno's erotic magic.

blowback from religious and civil authorities, however, and drove the traditions of magic far underground.

Their work was completed by the proponents of the scientific revolution, who denounced magic of all kinds just as heatedly as their religious rivals. As a result, the rebirth of a genuinely erotic magic in Western countries had to wait for the arrival of cultural influences from Asia, the recovery of lost teachings from the classical world, and the appearance of the force of nature named Paschal Beverly Randolph.

Sex magic

These days, Randolph is the most important figure in occult history most people have never heard of. The handful of modern historians who research the modern history of magic know all about him, and so do most serious ceremonial magicians, but he has been systematically erased from the history of magic in popular culture, and also from the writings associated with today's Neopagan movement. It is curious that this seems to be especially true among writers who make a point of parading their liberal credentials, because Randolph was the nineteenth century's most influential African-American occultist.[5]

He was born in 1825 in New York City's notorious Five Corners slum district and was orphaned by the age of five. At twelve he did what so many poor but ambitious boys did in those days, and took a job as cabin boy. On the brig *Phoebe*, he sailed the world around and rose to the rank of able seaman. When he left the sea after an injury in 1840, he worked as a barber to support himself while studying medicine.

In 1848, however, Randolph's career plans were disrupted when Spiritualism exploded onto the national stage. Randolph discovered that he had a remarkable gift for going into trance. That ability, combined with a magnetic personality, a quick mind, and a talent for oratory, made him an instant success in the Spiritualist circuit. He never looked back.

In 1853, as interest in Spiritualism was building in Europe, he sailed for England, where his lectures and seances drew large crowds and put him in touch with important figures in the British occult scene of the time. France proved just as hospitable. There he found an influential friend and supporter in the American general and alchemist

---

[5] Deveney 1997 is the standard modern biography of Randolph.

Ethan Allen Hitchcock, who brought him into high society and put him in contact with a branch of the Rosicrucian order. A little later he traveled in the Middle East. That was where, according to his later claims, he came into contact with a shaykh (spiritual teacher) of the al-Nusairi, a heretical Muslim sect in Syria.

That brought him into touch with a world of magical practice unknown at that time even to most serious occultists in the Western world. The fall of Rome and the rise of a puritanical, dogmatic form of Christianity in post-Roman Europe cut European cultures off from the fantastic wealth of magical and spiritual knowledge shared by the belt of ancient civilizations that extends from the Middle East through India to China. Some of that knowledge began to trickle back into Europe in the Middle Ages, but the erotic side of occultism remained largely shut out until Randolph's time. Whether it was from an al-Nusairi shaykh or from some other source, Randolph learned some of the secrets of sexual occultism that the East had to offer. He was not the only occultist who researched such things then or a little later, but he was one of the most influential.

When he returned to America in 1858, he brought with him a body of occult teaching and sexual lore that challenged some of the most rigid cultural assumptions of his time. It was a standard belief among physicians in the English-speaking world in the 1850s that women were incapable of sexual desire and that the female orgasm did not exist. Randolph taught, first, that women as well as men have sexual desires and are capable of orgasm; second, that orgasmic sexual release is essential to most people's physical and emotional health; third, that the male partner in heterosexual intercourse was responsible for helping the female partner achieve orgasm; and fourth, that the supreme magical act is a working in which the two partners in the sex act concentrate on the same intention at the moment of simultaneous orgasm, directing the creative power of the cosmos into the intention.

He called this last teaching the Ansairetic Arcanum, and said he had learned it from the al-Nusairi—"Ansaireh" was how the name of that sect was misspelled in English in his time. It became the secret teaching of the first documented Rosicrucian lodge in America, which Randolph founded in Boston in 1858, and the first documented American Rosicrucian order, the Third Temple of the Rosie Cross, which he founded in San Francisco in 1861.

The spread of his teachings was delayed by the roar of cannons at Fort Sumter that latter year, announcing the start of the Civil War.

Randolph responded to the outbreak of the war by shelving his magical activities and going to work full time recruiting African-American soldiers for the Union cause. As soon as the war was over, he moved to New Orleans and spent five years as a schoolteacher, passing on the skills of literacy to newly freed African-Americans. It was 1870 before he returned to teaching magic.

By then, however, alternative circles across the Western world were more than ready for what Randolph had to offer. Already in 1786 the English scholar Richard Payne Knight had scandalized the educated world of his day with a volume titled *A Discourse on the Worship of Priapus*, discussing the robust erotic symbolism of ancient Roman religion and its survivals in the Italian Catholicism of Knight's own time. More scholars followed in Knight's footsteps, showing that historic Christianity's profound unease toward sexuality marked it as an outlier among world religions, and exploring the ways that many other ancient and modern faiths included erotic symbolism and sexual activity in their own understandings of the sacred. Randolph's system of sex magic provided a practical expression of these same ideas. It was taken up enthusiastically in occult circles all over North America and Europe.

Sex was not the exclusive focus of Randolph's system of magic, to be sure. He taught exercises in clairvoyance using a magic mirror. He identified two kinds of clairvoyance—zorvoyance, which brought visions of what he called the "Middle Spaces," and aethaevoyance, which brought perceptions of what he called the "Ineffable Beyond." He divided every magical act into the three phases of Volantia, or calm focus; Decretism, the fixation of the whole will on a desired object; and Posism, or entering the silence. His students also took in a cosmology in which ours is one of forty-nine universes, and were taught what at the time was called the Pre-Adamite Theory—that is, the idea that human beings and the Earth itself had existed for more than the 6,000 years allotted them by literal interpretations of the Book of Genesis.

The rest of Randolph's busy and contentious life can be read in John Patrick Deveney's solid biography. The important point in terms of our story is that Randolph's life and writings made the magical dimensions of sex impossible to ignore from his time onward. His teachings were preserved and passed on by his student Freeman Dowd, who became the head of Randolph's Rosicrucian order after his teacher's untimely death, and spread from there to other occult societies and orders all across the Western world. To cite only two of many famous names, Aleister Crowley and his pupil Gerald Gardner, the inventor of the Neopagan religion of Wicca, both learned everything they knew about sex magic from lineages that ran straight back to Paschal Beverly Randolph.

More bodies than one

During these same years another current of occult theory and practice was helping to establish the foundations of polarity magic in a different way. Central to this second stream of magical lore were a series of challenging teachings that overturned standard Western ideas about the nature of human existence. Those teachings held that the material body of flesh and bone is only one of several bodies possessed by each human being; that the other bodies occupy the same space but are composed of different modes of substance; that these other bodies are involved in human sexuality and other forms of interpersonal interaction, along with the material body; that these other bodies have sexual polarity like the material body—and that the polarities of the other bodies are not necessarily the same as that of the material body.

The awareness that human beings have subtle bodies in addition to the material body goes back a very long way. Ancient Egyptian priests and priestesses taught that each person had, alongside the material body, several other bodies, including the *ba* or spirit-body and the *ka* or life-body. The mystics and mages of ancient Greece spoke learnedly of the *ochema pneuma* or body of life force and the *augoeides ochema* or body of light. In Egypt and Greece, and in many other ancient cultures besides, the main focus of this branch of occult lore was in preparing for death and the afterlife. Centuries passed before the role of the subtle bodies in life, rather than death, became a central concern of occult practitioners in the Western world.

This shift was largely the work of Helena Petrovna Blavatsky, the extraordinary Russian mage who launched the first public organization for teaching occultism in modern times. HPB, as her students liked to call her, spent the first half of her life studying occult teachings in various corners of the world, and the second half passing them on to eager audiences in the United States, India, and England. The Theosophical Society, which she helped to found and then ran for many years, became the most popular venue for occult instruction across the Western world all through the late nineteenth and early twentieth centuries.

The existence of subtle bodies was a central theme of Theosophical instruction. In the early days of the Theosophical Society, most authors followed Blavatsky's lead and used a set of terms borrowed from Sanskrit for the subtle bodies. Early in the twentieth century, however, most Theosophical writers took to using more straightforward labels for the different sheaths or vestures of the self: the physical or material body, the etheric body or etheric double, the astral body, and the mental body or mental sheath. These terms will be used in this book, and are defined and discussed at length in Chapter 4.

It's common for writers these days who have uncritically adopted modern materialist ideology to dismiss talk about the subtle bodies as "woo-woo." Here again, though, we're face to face with the ukelele players from the metaphor in Chapter 1, for whom words like "andante" and "allegro non troppo" are so much gobbledygook. Among the training exercises that prepare a student for ceremonial magic are exercises that awaken the ability to perceive the subtle bodies, or more precisely to recognize that we experience them all the time but have been taught to discount and ignore our own perceptions. These same exercises develop certain energy centers in the subtle bodies, which function as organs of perception and action on the corresponding planes.

Exercises of these kinds were taught in the Theosophical Society to members of the Esoteric Section, the inner circle of the Society. As the occult revival kickstarted by Randolph and Blavatsky hit its stride, other exercises were brought in from a wide range of spiritual traditions, or created by innovative occultists, and spread throughout the occult community of the time. Meanwhile a basic knowledge of the subtle bodies became widespread, not least because Theosophical authors such as Arthur A. Powell penned entire books on the subject.

Practical applications of this knowledge did not take long to emerge. Already in 1855, Alphonse Louis Constant—who wrote under the pen name Eliphas Lévi—had revolutionized occult philosophy across the Western world in his book *Doctrine and Ritual of High Magic*, which reinterpreted older magical practices in terms of the movements of the life force.

Three generations of mages, working along the lines Lévi sketched out, explored ways of concentrating and directing the life force using the tools of will and imagination. The role of erotic energies in this process received some attention, but it was only one of many factors considered by the early investigators in the field. It would take a later generation of occultists, drawing on these and other bodies of lore, to create modern polarity magic.

Sublimating the forces

Another current that flowed into the creation of polarity magic also came by way of Blavatsky's efforts to rekindle the flame of occult knowledge in the Western world. Much of the material she introduced to students in Europe and the Americas came from India, and even more of it was given a coat of Indian terminology in order to benefit from popular Western notions about "the Mystic East." It is largely due to her efforts that Westerners became interested in concepts such as reincarnation and karma. That interest paved the way for the arrival and acceptance of qualified Hindu, Buddhist, and Sikh teachers in Western countries during the century following Blavatsky's death.

One of the Indian spiritual concepts that attracted the most interest in the West in the immediate wake of Blavatsky's career was kundalini. This is one of the many forms of *prana*, the life energy. In most people it is latent, hidden away in an energy center at the base of the spine. Under certain conditions it can be awakened, and once this happens it rises up the spine, passing through a series of other energy centers in the spine and brain, until it reaches the center at the top of the skull. Done in a carefully controlled manner, this process is among the fastest ways to achieve the mystical states of consciousness Western writers call "enlightenment." If it is released without the necessary safeguards, however, it can wreck the nervous system of the practitioner and cause severe illness or death.

Blavatsky and the first generation or so of her pupils understood the potential dangers of kundalini but did not have the training needed to work with it successfully. The Theosophical Society in their time accordingly taught a great deal of occult philosophy but only the most basic forms of occult practice, encouraging students to practice a few simple forms of meditation while warning about more advanced techniques in colorful language. In the long run, this was probably a good strategy, as it helped lay a solid foundation on which occult and mystical teachings could build in the century that followed.

At the time, however, it had embarrassing results. One of the great problems was that Theosophy came of age in the wake of the Victorian era and thus inevitably shared some of that era's obsessive ideas about sex. Blavatsky and other early Theosophical writers such as

C.W. Leadbeater recognized that kundalini was not simply sexual in nature, but a great many other figures in the movement lost track of this point. The idea that strict celibacy all by itself would lead to exalted spiritual states, a commonplace of certain Western mystical traditions since the Middle Ages, found its way into the resulting mix. It seems never to have occurred to the teachers who promoted this approach that the energies of sex had to be given somewhere else to go, or they would sooner or later find the usual outlet.

American occultist Max Freedom Long penned a wry account of his youthful experiences with this sort of Theosophical training for a 1946 issue of *The Flying Roll*, the magazine of the Borderland Sciences Research Association. In 1915, under the guidance of a Theosophical teacher, he took up daily exercises in meditation and concentration, a vegetarian diet, a strict program of moral improvement, and complete celibacy, including an attempt to prevent all seminal emissions. The results were not what Theosophical literature had promised. Plagued by sexual dreams that resulted in orgasm, he made a pressure-sensitive collar for his penis and hooked it to a buzzer, so that the contraption would wake him from his dreams if he had an erection. This cost him a great deal of sleep. No supernormal powers showed themselves, nor did kundalini awaken, and the experiment finally ground to a halt when his erotic dreams started ending in orgasm without an erection full enough to set off the buzzer![6]

Long was far from the only person to have such equivocal results from Theosophical training. As a result, alternative occult movements throughout the Western world experimented with less limited approaches to practice. Experiences such as Long's led many of these experimenters to recognize that it is not enough to bottle up sexual energies—they have to be redirected and put to some other use. Various methods of sublimating sexual forces were tested and circulated among occultists during the first decades of the twentieth century, and some of these provided material for the eventual synthesis that created polarity magic.

Sex with spirits

Along with sex magic, a knowledge of the subtle bodies, and the explorations of various methods for sublimating erotic energies, a fourth and considerably more exotic body of lore that influenced polarity magic

---

[6] His account is in Long 1946.

came by way of the tradition of erotic liaisons between human beings and spirits. This tradition goes back far into antiquity. It has been traditional in many tribal cultures since ancient times for shamans to marry their guardian spirits, and the marriages in question include erotic interactions. For that matter, the idea that gods and spirits could not merely have sex with human beings but father or bear children as a result is found in most of the world's mythologies—the Christian teaching that Jesus was the child of Mary and the Holy Spirit, conceived without a physical sexual liaison, has many less prim analogues around the world.

The medieval Christian church, less ignorant of magic than its successors, treated sex between human beings and spirits as a sin rather than an impossibility, and witches were accused of having sex with demons as part of their orgiastic festivals. Historian of religions Carlo Ginzburg has suggested that many accusations leveled at witches by inquisitors during the years of the witchcraft panic were based on misunderstandings of shamanistic beliefs that had survived in Europe from ancient times.[7] Certainly the archaic tradition of sex with spirits was far from extinct during the Renaissance rebirth of ancient magical traditions. The great German mage and alchemist Paracelsus, in his 1566 book *Liber de Nymphiis, Sylphiis, Pygmaeis et Salamandris et Caeteris Spiritibus* (*The Book of Nymphs, Sylphs, Pygmies, Salamanders, and Other Spirits*), recounted numerous examples of erotic liaisons between humans and spiritual beings.

The nineteenth-century revival of magic found its way to the concept of sex with spirits promptly enough. One of the major inspirations for nineteenth- and twentieth-century occult explorations along these lines was a lively French novel, *Le Comte de Gabalis*, written by Abbé Nicholas-Pierre-Henri Montfaucon de Villars and first published in 1670. The influence of this novel is all the more remarkable because *Le Comte de Gabalis* is a work of satire that makes fun of the occult scene of Montfaucon de Villars' own time. Its ribald theme is the tongue-in-cheek claim that the whole point of magic is having hot sex with elemental spirits.[8]

Humor is one of the tools of the operative occultist, however. Earlier in the seventeenth century the alchemist Michael Maier published books with titles like *Lusus Serius* (*A Serious Game*) and *Jocus Severus* (*A Severe Jest*), which communicated complicated alchemical recipes in the form of deliberately silly stories. Not long before Maier

---

[7] See Ginzburg 1991.
[8] Nagel 2007 is a useful guide to *Le Comte de Gabalis* and its enduring influence.

wrote, the anonymous German authors of the Rosicrucian manifestoes wielded edgy humor as part of their project to foster a political and spiritual revival of Europe. These and other examples led nineteenth- and twentieth-century occultists in Europe and the Americas to treat Montfaucon de Villars' novel as an attempt to communicate important occult secrets under the cover of raucous humor. It is indicative that even today the most widely available English translation of *Le Comte de Gabalis*, made by American occultist Sarah Emery "Lotus" Dudley and first published in 1914, includes a detailed and earnest commentary by the translator that interprets the novel as a serious work of Rosicrucian occult instruction.

Two influential American figures in the alternative spirituality move- ment of the time, Thomas Lake Harris and Ida Craddock, also took up the idea of sex with spirits and made it central to their respective teachings. Harris is nearly forgotten today, but his Brotherhood of the New Life had a massive influence on the occult community in his time. His teach- ings about erotic relationships with spirits found their way to British occult circles by way of Dr. Edmund Berridge, an influential member of the Hermetic Order of the Golden Dawn who was also active in Harris's group. Berridge, under the pen name Respiro, wrote a series of pam- phlets on the teachings of the Brotherhood that were widely circulated in the British occult scene all through the early twentieth century.

Ida Craddock is a little more widely remembered today because of her importance as a pioneering feminist and advocate of birth control. The aggressively secular nature of so much of twentieth-century femi- nism, however, led a great many otherwise careful writers to ignore Craddock's longtime involvement in alternative spirituality, and espe- cially her advocacy of love affairs with spirits as an alternative to the often difficult realities of sex and marriage in late nineteenth-century America. Though Craddock was a scandalous figure in her time, her teachings and ideas found audiences in occult circles for many decades after her death in 1903.

All this may seem to have little enough in common with the polarity magic this book teaches, but the connection is real and important. Since spirits lack material bodies, their sexual interactions with human beings must take place through the subtle bodies discussed by the Theosophical and occult authors mentioned earlier. That led occultists to explore the possibility that human beings could exchange erotic energies through these same subtle channels—the insight central to polarity magic.

By the time Dion Fortune and her associates began developing polarity magic in its modern form, in other words, most of the preparatory work had already been done for them. Randolph and his successors had explored the magical dimensions of sexuality; Blavatsky and her successors had explored the subtle bodies and their practical uses in occultism; a great many practitioners in Blavatsky's wake had explored the possibilities of sublimating erotic energies; and the writers who followed the path opened up by *The Comte de Gabalis* had explored the non-physical side of sex. What remained to be done was the development of a synthesis, and Dion Fortune provided that.

Dion Fortune

Her real name was Violet Mary Firth, and she was born in 1890 to a middle-class family in Britain. A childhood interest in Christian mysticism, fostered by exposure to the Christian Science church via her mother, gave way a little later on to a fascination with Theosophy and other forms of occultism. Beginning in 1917, she studied with Dr. Theodore Moriarty, a respected occultist of the time, and was initiated into his magical lodge in 1919. In that same year she also became a member of one of the offshoots of the Hermetic Order of the Golden Dawn, the most prestigious magical organization of early twentieth-century Britain. Eventually she decided to pursue her own path, and in 1922 she founded a magical order, the Fraternity of the Inner Light.[9]

Like many occultists of her time, she was deeply interested in the revolution in psychology launched around the time of her birth by the Austrian physician Sigmund Freud. In 1914, when Freudian psychoanalysis was still a fringe movement and analysts were not yet required to get university degrees in psychology, she studied at the Medico-Psychological Clinic at Brunswick Square, London, one of the centers of Freudian practice in England at that time. She qualified as a lay analyst and practiced at the Clinic for a short time. The lure of magic was too strong, and she left the Clinic to become a full-time occult teacher and author, but Freud's focus on sexuality as a core issue in human psychology stayed with her to the end of her life.

Polarity magic was only one of several branches of magical practice where Fortune and her inner circle of associates broke new ground.

---

[9] Now the Society of the Inner Light.

They showed that the complex and cumbersome degree rituals of the Golden Dawn could be replaced by a simpler degree system with good results. They explored the use of the creative imagination in occultism, developing several modes of practice that remain central to ceremonial magic to this day. They launched a Christian religious body, the Guild of the Master Jesus, which pioneered an approach to Christian worship that will be discussed in a later chapter. They organized an occult network to defend Britain from Nazi magical workings in the perilous early years of the Second World War. They also took part in one of the great projects of early twentieth-century occultism—the attempt to use clairvoyance to gain accurate information about the distant past—and got the same highly equivocal results as Rudolf Steiner, Max Heindel, and other participants in that effort.

These days, though, most people who know about Dion Fortune associate her with the magical dimensions of sexuality. Partly this association comes from two of her earliest occult works, *The Esoteric Philosophy of Love and Marriage* (1924) and *The Problem of Purity* (1927, but based on material she first drafted as lectures in 1916). Both of these accepted the standard sexual morality of Fortune's own place and time, treating any sexual activity outside of heterosexual marriage as a moral and social error. *The Esoteric Philosophy of Love and Marriage* set out a general theory of sex on occult lines; *The Problem of Purity* offered help, using simple magical means, to those people who wanted to follow the accepted sexual morality just mentioned but had to corral their own unruly desires to do so. The latter book includes a simple method of redirecting and sublimating sexual energies: evidence that her thoughts were already moving in the direction that would give rise to polarity work.

Far more influential in shaping Fortune's modern reputation for sexual occultism was her tetralogy of four magical novels, *The Winged Bull* (1935), *The Goat-Foot God* (1936), *The Sea Priestess* (1938), and *Moon Magic* (posthumously published in 1957). In these, according to her own testimony, Fortune set out to communicate to her readers the experience of magical initiation, and succeeded in that bold attempt as well as anyone ever has. Close reading of these four novels, combined with imaginative work with the imagery they contain, is in fact an effective way of initiation into magic.[10] Yet all four books also focus on romantic and erotic relationships between men and women.

---

[10] This has been explored very capably in Billington and Rees 2022.

The main characters in each novel are a man and a woman who are drawn into a relationship that is as much magical as romantic. In the first two novels, the relationship leads to marriage and, by inference, sex; in the last two, the relationship stays physically unconsummated but magically potent. Quite a bit of the theory and practice of polarity magic finds its way into all four novels. At the same time, there is another dimension to all four stories, one that overlaps with polarity magic but needs to be distinguished from it.

Fortune's psychoanalytic training, her experience as a teacher in the occult counterculture between the wars, and the problems with her own marriage (which ended in divorce at a time when that was still legally and socially difficult) led her to focus attention on the shamefaced and miserable mess that so many British people made of their erotic lives in the post-Victorian era. She understood, as her contemporary Aleister Crowley never did, that changing the attitudes of a culture cannot be done by rejecting those attitudes outright and flaunting one's violations of the usual code of conduct. Her approach to changing the unsatisfactory sexual culture of her time has been well characterized as "socially responsible sex magic"—an approach to the erotic dimensions of magic that avoided a direct rupture with the conventional ideas of her time, but changed them gradually from within by seeding new ideas and insights into the collective imagination of her culture.[11]

Being a capable mage, Fortune set out to accomplish this through the systematic invocation of a carefully chosen pair of divine archetypes: Isis and Pan. Her four magical novels were part of this project, but they were not the whole of it. Fortune and other members of the Fraternity of the Inner Light also took what was then the radical step of performing a set of rituals open to people outside the Fraternity. The Rites of Isis and Pan aimed at restoring the connections that link the spiritual realms of existence with feminine and masculine erotic energies. To judge from the published texts of the Rites, they must have been remarkable experiences for the participants and the audience alike.

The point to keep in mind, however, is that the reorientation of British sexual culture Fortune pursued was one practical application of polarity magic, not a central part of the method of polarity work. While British sex life doubtless still has its share of problems, the culture

---

[11] I have taken the phrase "socially responsible sex magic" from van Raalte 2015, which discusses this aspect of Fortune's work in detail.

of severe erotic repression that burdened so many women's lives in Fortune's time is mostly a thing of the past. The novels still have their value as a means of magical self-initiation; the Rites of Isis and Pan, now that they have been published,[12] are a valuable resource for ritual designers; but these applications of polarity work are no longer as central to the work of the polarity mage as they arguably needed to be in Fortune's own time. That project succeeded, and it's possible to go on in new directions.

Twilight and dawn

Dion Fortune was born as the culture of Victorian puritanism was cracking apart, and she died just before the first stirrings of the sexual revolution got under way. Her era was therefore a propitious time for explorations of the subtle dimensions of sex. For that matter, she was far from the only occultist of her time to test some of the possibilities of sublimated erotic energy in magic. Even devout Christian occultists such as Arthur Edward Waite and his student Charles Williams wrote about that theme, Waite at great and turgid length in his book *The Holy Kabbalah*, Williams indirectly in his novels but far more explicitly in an unguarded passage in one of his nonfiction works.[13]

According to some later sources, some initiates of the Fraternity of the Inner Light also practiced sex magic in the strict sense of the word, with physical intercourse taking place at the culmination of the working. That was experimental in nature, part of the Fraternity's efforts to push forward the boundaries of magical knowledge and practice. Fortune herself seems to have believed that polarity magic was more appropriate to the conditions of her time and place than sex magic, but she left that choice among many others to the participants themselves.

Fortune died in 1946. In the years immediately following her death, the methods of polarity magic she pioneered remained in use in the British occult scene, and also spread to some occult schools elsewhere. One example is the Builders of the Adytum (BOTA), an influential American occult order founded by Paul Foster Case. This order included in its curriculum a course in sexual polarity workings written by Case's successor Ann Davies, which shows considerable influence from Fortune's work.

---

[12] Knight 2013.
[13] Williams 1941, pp. 231–2.

Other, less widely known occult schools also took up polarity work of various types. The practical methods included in this book come from one such source, an assortment of American occult traditions I received from my teacher John Gilbert between 2003 and 2010.

The sexual revolution of the 1960s drove the entire subject of polarity magic onto the sidelines, however. Occultists who came of age in the wake of the Sixties by and large didn't see any difference between sublimating erotic energies and suppressing them. Sex magic of various kinds, nearly all of it following the methods pioneered by P.B. Randolph, accordingly took centerstage in large parts of the occult community. The Ordo Templi Orientis, revived and promoted by Aleister Crowley's student Grady McMurtry, played a large part in making sex magic popular, but an even larger role was taken by Gardnerian Wicca and its many offshoots and imitations. Ceremonies performed in the nude, and ritual intercourse ("the Great Rite") as the central sacrament of the tradition, appealed powerfully to the sensibilities of the time. In that context it was easy to dismiss polarity magic, and the rest of Dion Fortune's pioneering work with sublimated erotic energies, as nothing more than Victorian moralizing in magical guise.

Times change, however, and the mandatory promiscuity that followed in the wake of the Sixties seems to many people today just as artificial and burdensome as the mandatory prudery of the Victorian era. In the broad and flexible space between these extremes, polarity magic is one of the options for occult practitioners, and it is high time that the techniques of polarity work be made available to ceremonial magicians who choose to use them.

This is easier now than it once was in view of another factor. In recent years, many of Dion Fortune's previously unpublished writings have seen print. Many other once-secret magical writings from the late nineteenth and early twentieth centuries have likewise become available to students, and the softening of academic prejudices against occultism means that capable works of scholarship on these and older magical traditions are easier to find than ever before. Methods of working magic using sublimated erotic energies are available now for those who want to use them. This book explains one way in which this can be done.

CHAPTER 3

Polarity in the macrocosm

One of the reasons that polarity magic has been so poorly understood in recent years is that some of the prejudices and preconceptions of contemporary Western industrial society get in the way of a clear grasp of its principles. This is true of the entire tradition of ceremonial magic, of course. The world that modern scientific materialism insists we all live in is a world with no room for magic—and there are potent political reasons for this act of exclusion.

Magic is above all the power of the individual. It unfolds from the mage's own self-knowledge and self-mastery, and can be wielded only by one who is willing to stand apart from the entanglements of collective consciousness and the pressures of unthinking obedience to social hierarchies. One of the lessons of history is that those who achieve self-control cannot reliably be controlled by anyone else. This makes the practice of self-control unwelcome to those who aspire to be rulers and masters of the rest of us. The denunciations of magic that come from the mouthpieces of today's establishment, and the would-be establishments of some politically ambitious countercultures, have this at their root.

While all forms of ceremonial magic come in for this sort of hostility, polarity magic fields more of it than most magical arts. Partly this is because self-knowledge and self-mastery are especially important in polarity work, since erotic energies have a stronger pull on human consciousness and will than almost any other factor. Partly, though, it is because polarity magic requires a reinterpretation of the entire range of human erotic experience. Modern materialism and traditional religious beliefs in the Western world both treat sexuality as though it belongs entirely to what mages call the material plane. Polarity magic, by contrast, works with dimensions of erotic experience that extend beyond the limits of matter, and rise up to the realm of the spiritual. By doing this, it violates some of the most deeply held taboos of our culture.

This and the chapters to come will speak of some length about erotic energy, and about masculine and feminine energies, the two polarized forms of erotic energy. It is worth pointing out here that these are not the kinds of energies that physicists can measure, though anyone who has ever experienced sexual arousal knows that erotic energies can have remarkable effects on the plane of matter, especially but not only through the medium of human bodies. The word "energy" in this context is therefore a metaphor, but a very useful one.

This metaphor makes it easier for the student of polarity magic to think of erotic experience in terms of pressure, flow, charge, and discharge. It also helps the student avoid the trap of thinking of erotic experience in a purely material sense. As we will see, the subtle presence we call erotic energy can build up, flow outward, and be drawn inward on several different planes of human experience. In doing this, it shows its twofold nature in ways that are central to the work ahead.

Dinergy

Of the concepts that must be grasped to make sense of polarity magic, perhaps the most important of all is the principle of *dinergy*. The word "dinergy" was introduced by architect and sacred geometer György Doczi in his 1981 book *The Power of Limits*. It comes from the Latin prefix *di-*, "two," and the word "energy," and it makes a convenient label for the process by which beauty, power, and magic emerge from the interaction of two essentially different energies, forces, or factors, one of which is active, the other receptive.

Consider the exquisite curves made by tall grass in the wind. The wind here is the active factor, the grass the receptive factor. Each affects and is affected by the other, and beauty results. Apply the same principle to the relation between the wind and the sails and rigging of a sailboat, and if you do so with sufficient skill, you get the sail's elegant curves and the motive power that sends the boat skimming across the water.

Two points should be noted here. First, dinergy requires a relationship between different factors in a polarity relationship; you cannot get the same effect by bringing together two factors of the same kind. Two breezes or two sails put together won't propel a boat! One factor provides the motive force, the other provides a measured resistance that channels the force into power and beauty. Each has its own function, which is complementary to the function of the other, and the polarity between them makes dinergy happen.

Second, the two factors need to be approximately equal for dinergy to flourish. If the wind is too weak for the sail, the sail hangs limp and the boat does not move. If the wind is too strong for the sail, the sail tears, and once again the boat does not move. Each needs to be scaled to the other, and neither one dominates the process.

The principle of dinergy can be applied to a great many things. The philosophy of Taoism, in fact, is based on dinergy, with yang as the active principle and yin as the receptive principle, unfolding in polarity throughout the universe in a constantly changing dance of complementary energies. In the practice of polarity magic, dinergy is essential, because it defines the relationship between masculine and feminine energies within each person, between two or more people, and throughout the cosmos as a whole.

Please note: masculine and feminine *energies*, not individuals. It is essential, to make any kind of sense of polarity magic, to realize that no human being is entirely masculine or entirely feminine. Each of us embodies both masculine and feminine energies, and each of us interacts with other people through exchanges of both these energies. How this works is a complex process in which dinergy plays a central part, and the practical implications of that process will be set out in detail in the next chapter. In this chapter we are exploring the role of masculine and feminine energies in the universe as a whole.

Traditional occult philosophy has a distinctive way of speaking about the universe and its relationship to the individual. In occult writings the universe is very often called the macrocosm, literally "big universe," while the individual human being is called the microcosm, literally "little universe." Central to occult teaching is the recognition that these two mirror each other. This shouldn't be taken in a simpleminded or literal sense—as Plato pointed out a long time ago, the universe doesn't have feet!—but it expresses a crucial truth. We and the universe we live in are born of the same substance, after all, and we are subject to the same natural laws.

The balance of matter, mind, and spirit in the human microcosm reflects a similar balance in the macrocosm. The flow of erotic energies through each of us, and between individuals as well, mirrors the flow of comparable energies through the cosmos as a whole. The mirroring of macrocosm and microcosm allows us to understand ourselves more completely by understanding the universe around us.

The planes of being

To ceremonial mages, as already discussed above, the universe consists of much more than physical matter and energy. It can best be understood as a matrix of multiple kinds, states, or (as traditional occultists like to say) planes of being. These planes are not stacked on top of one another like geological strata, say, or dishes in a cupboard. They interpenetrate each other and fill the entire cosmos. Think of the way that air, sound, and light are all present in the room where you are sitting right now. This is a good metaphor for the way that the different planes are all simultaneously present in every place.

The idea of different planes of being can seem very strange at first glance. What you may not realize is that you already perceive three of these planes, and parts of a fourth. The material plane is the one you perceive with your five ordinary senses: sight, hearing, touch, taste, and smell. This is the plane of matter and energy that scientists study, and the description of that plane offered by modern scientists is on the whole accepted by most ceremonial mages. The problem with modern science from an occult standpoint is not that it's inaccurate—it's that it's incomplete. Science fails to give a complete view of existence because it leaves the other planes of being out of consideration, and these other planes are essential parts of the universe that human beings experience.

The plane closest in nature to the material plane is called the etheric plane. This is the plane of the life force. You experience the ether whenever you walk into an unfamiliar place and feel what members of a certain generation used to call the "vibe" of the place or the people in it. You sense actions on the etheric plane when a prickle at the back of your neck tells you that someone behind you is staring at you.

It's by way of the substance of the etheric plane—*qi* in Chinese and *ki* in Japanese and Korean—that traditional martial artists perform their feats, and acupuncturists heal illnesses. People in many other cultures make equally constructive use of the normal, healthy human ability to sense the etheric plane. Most people in the Western industrial nations, by contrast, are bullied and shamed in childhood to make them stop paying attention to their own perceptions of the etheric plane. If they take up the study and practice of ceremonial magic, they have to unlearn those childhood habits and start noticing their etheric environment.

One step further beyond the etheric plane lies the astral plane, the plane of imagination, feeling, and desire. You experience the astral plane every night in your dreams, whether you remember them or not. You also experience the astral plane every time you imagine something, remember something, or think of something. Most of what Western people call their inner life takes place on the astral plane, taking forms that resemble sensory experience but do not pass through the material senses. Right now, before reading any further, take a moment to remember your phone number. Did you see it written in your mind's eye, or hear an imaginary voice speaking it, or feel imaginary fingers tapping out the numbers on a screen or a keypad? All those inner experiences are modes of astral perception, and all three of them play an important role in ceremonial magic.

One more step beyond the astral plane is the mental plane. It's easy to misunderstand this plane because human beings are not yet very good at perceiving it. The mental plane is not the plane of thoughts, it's the plane of meanings. Consider the word *Backpfeifengesicht*. If you don't happen to know German, it's simply a string of letters. You can memorize it a letter at a time, or you can have someone say it for you, learn that it's pronounced "back-FIFE-en-geh-SIKH-t," and memorize that sequence of sounds. All this is in the realms of experience that mages call the astral and material planes: the astral plane when you repeat it silently in your mind, the material plane when you say it out loud or write it.

Then you learn that in German, it means "a face that just begs to be punched." All at once that sequence of letters and sounds takes on a new dimension—a dimension of meaning. Doubtless you can think of people you know who deserve to be described this way! Their faces, not to mention their annoying expressions and irritating habits, all become part of your understanding of the meaning of *Backpfeifengesicht*.

That sense of meaning belongs to the mental plane, which is for us the plane of connections and abstract relationships.

The mental plane goes far beyond this, but once again, human beings have not yet evolved the ability to perceive the further reaches of that plane. There are also planes beyond the mental plane—the spiritual, causal, and divine planes—which we cannot yet perceive at all. (We know about them because over the centuries, certain sages and mystics have reached the point at which it is possible to glimpse the higher planes, or communicate with spiritual beings who can perceive those planes.) The four planes we can perceive—the material, etheric, astral, and mental planes—are the ones that play roles in polarity magic. The accompanying table will help sort out the planes discussed in this book.[14]

Plane:	Nature and Function:
Mental	plane of meanings, intentions, and values
Astral	plane of dreams, imagination, and desires
Etheric	plane of life force and of intuitive senses
Material	plane of physical matter and energy

Ordinary human life includes experiences on all four of these planes. In the societies of the modern industrial West, we are taught that only one of them—the material plane—is objectively real, while the other planes exist solely inside certain lumps of meat called human brains. To the ceremonial mage, things are not so simpleminded as that. Knowing that the other planes also exist in their own right, the mage can learn to perceive what is happening on all four planes, and can also learn to take action on any or all of them. This, in turn, makes it possible under certain circumstances to shape events on one plane by taking action on another.

Magic and the planes

An important occult axiom holds that "the planes are discrete and not continuous." This means that each plane has its own laws and phenomena, and the rules that govern one plane may not function on another. It also means that what happens on one plane does not necessarily spill

---

[14] Dion Fortune used a different set of labels for the planes. There are several taxonomies of the planes, each of which has its own strengths and weaknesses. The one used in this book is the one I use in my magical writings more generally. I have found it particularly useful for making sense of practical magic.

over onto another. We all know this from personal experience, of course. If you want to get to the other side of a locked door, your imagination will not do the job by itself—you need a key, or perhaps a sledgehammer, both of which exist and function on the same material plane of existence as the door itself.

The planes are not totally isolated from each other, however. Again, this is a matter of personal experience. Your imagination, which belongs to the astral plane, can direct your vital energy, which belongs to the etheric plane, to activate your muscles to put the key in the lock or swing the sledgehammer against the door. One of the central themes of occult philosophy is that there are certain points of contact between the planes, and influences can pass from plane to plane through these points of contact. As the example just given may have already suggested to you, conscious individual beings like you and me are among the most important of these points.

The points of contact between the planes are of crucial importance because the material plane, the realm of matter and energy known to modern science, is a plane of effects, not of causes. Everything that exists on the material plane is a result of causes on what, metaphorically, we can call the higher planes. According to occult philosophy, in fact, the process by which all things come into being begins on the divine plane and cascades down the planes from there until it finally reaches manifestation on the material plane.

This is the principle behind all operative occultism. Human beings are not limited to the material plane. We also perceive the etheric plane, the astral plane, and part of the mental plane. Furthermore, if we learn how to do so, we can act on each of these planes. It is because we can perceive patterns coming down the planes before they manifest in matter that we are capable of anticipating the future through divination. It is because we can act on the planes to shape patterns as they descend toward matter that we are capable of shaping the future through magic. All the tools and techniques of divination and magic, from tarot cards and crystal balls to ritual daggers and magic wands, are simply ways to help the human mind perceive and shape the descending patterns of the higher planes.

Solar and telluric currents

Speaking of the mental, astral, and etheric planes as "higher" is a metaphor, of course. All the planes of existence are present everywhere and interpenetrate each other, and so the mental plane (for example) is as much below the material plane, beside it, around it, and within it, as above it. As students of occultism develop the ability to perceive the flow of the life force around them, however, they typically become aware of two primary sources of that force—the sun and the earth—which provide a vertical dimension for the flow of life, magic, and power in the world. It's for this reason that certain occult teachings describe a solar current that descends from above and a telluric current that rises up from below.[15]

The solar current comes gets its name because it comes from the sun. It flows through interplanetary space to the earth's upper atmosphere, where it spreads out and descends to the surface. It increases and decreases in any given place according to the position of the sun in the sky. It is strongest at dawn and noon, but it is present even at midnight; it flows wherever light from the sky can reach, and penetrates a short distance down into the soil. The other planets of the solar system reflect the solar current to earth just as they reflect the sun's light, and their interactions with the solar current are the sources of the influences that are tracked by astrology. The solar current's traditional symbols in myth and legend are birds such as the eagle, the hawk, and the heron. Occult writings call it *aud* or *od*. It is symbolically masculine, and one of its names is the current of knowledge.

The telluric current gets its name because it rises from the center of the earth. It passes through the crust to the surface, and it is shaped by place the way the solar current is shaped by time; this is why certain places are more sacred than others, and certain places are the sites of more uncanny events than others. Underground water affects the telluric current very strongly. Springs and wells where water comes to the surface bring this current through to the surface at high intensity. So do large healthy trees, whose roots draw up water from underground. The serpent and the dragon are the most common symbols of the telluric current in myth and legend. Its names in occult lore include the secret fire, the dragon current, and *aub* or *ob*. It is symbolically feminine, and one of its names is the current of power.

Ceremonial mages, as an essential part of their training, learn to draw on one or both of these currents in order to work their magic. The current or currents used in magic vary from one system of ceremonial magic to another. Some systems use the solar current alone,

---

[15] The word "telluric" comes from Tellus, an old name for the earth.

while others work only with the telluric current. Still others work with both currents. The practical methods given in this book work with both the solar and telluric currents, though methods for using just one of the currents are included for readers who practice other magical systems.

As with anything else, there are tradeoffs involved in the choice of which current or currents to use in magic. Systems of ceremonial magic that use only one current are simpler to master and practice, and they allow a more intensive focus on certain specific goals: for example, systems of ceremonial magic that work with the solar current alone often get faster results when used for the purposes of personal transformation and spiritual development, while systems that work with the telluric current alone often get faster results when used for personal and planetary healing. Working with both currents requires more patience, but it opens the way to a possibility that work with one current alone cannot reach: the creation and activation of a third current, which is sometimes called the lunar current.

The lunar current does not exist under ordinary conditions in the individual human being or in the world. It has to be made by the fusion of the solar and telluric currents. It is shaped neither by space nor by time but by states of consciousness. Its symbols in myth and legend include the egg, the jewel, the sacred cup, and the child, and it is called *aur* or *or* in occult writings; it is also one of the secrets behind the legend of the Holy Grail. When it awakens in an individual, it opens up the inner senses and grants wisdom, revelation, and enlightenment. When it awakens in the land—a far more difficult task, but one that was once done quite regularly in the days when magic was known and practiced by ancient priests and priestesses—it brings fertility and plenty.

Both the solar and telluric currents, as we will see in the chapters to come, have significant parts to play in polarity workings. The lunar current, "the wondrous child and jewel of light,"[16] also has a role, and can be brought into manifestation by means of polarity magic. In the chapters of this book that discuss the practice of advanced polarity magic, one method for doing this will be given in detail; other methods can readily be devised by the experienced mage.

---

[16] This is a quote from a Universal Gnostic Church communion ritual, which invokes the three currents.

Creation and evolution

The solar and telluric currents are specialized forms of a much more general pattern which is well known in occult philosophy and constantly used in magical practice. As noted earlier in this chapter, the material plane is understood in occultism as a realm of effects. Everything that takes place there is set in motion by patterns descending from higher planes, and ultimately from the divine plane. Just as the solar current is balanced by the telluric current, however, this downward flow of creative force from spirit to matter is balanced by an upward flow of created forms from matter to spirit. Thus the movement of creation is balanced by an equal and opposite movement of evolution.

Textbooks of occult philosophy discuss these paired flows in detail because they have a very direct application to the nature, origin, and destiny of the human soul. Each of us, in the occult vision of reality, came into existence out of a current of creative energy descending from the divine plane into matter. At the lowest point of the descending arc, that current unfolded itself into individual souls, each of which then began rising back up through the planes through many lives, first in mineral or elemental forms, then in vegetable bodies, then in animal bodies. The human level is a transition from the animal realm to another, less material form of embodiment, and there are further modes beyond that, until each of us reaches full maturity as a being capable of experiencing and acting on all the planes of existence.

The same principle, however, applies on many other scales and in many other contexts. Each magical working, for example, involves a descent and ascent of the same kind. The power that makes magic function descends from the divine plane—this is why ceremonial mages invoke the divine using traditional holy names and words of power in their workings—and completes the creative movement on the material plane—this is why every magical working has some material basis, even if this is no more than movements of the mage's material body in ritual. From there, the influence set in motion by the working rises back up the planes, shaping the consciousness of the mage, and ultimately becoming part of the process by which the universe as a whole awakens to an awareness of its own nature and potential.

Human sexual reproduction, the most important form of polarity working on the material plane, follows the same pattern. Occultists of an older generation liked to point out that male genitals extend downward and outward, and the male body typically tapers from the shoulders to the hips, as though forming an arrow pointing down; female genitals, by contrast, extend upward and inward, and the female body typically tapers from the hips to the shoulders, as though forming an arrow pointing up. This shows, according to the traditional lore, that the male body is specialized to bring the descending current down into physical generation, while the female body is specialized to receive that current and give it the physical form that will allow it to ascend: in English, after all, we still speak of "raising a child."

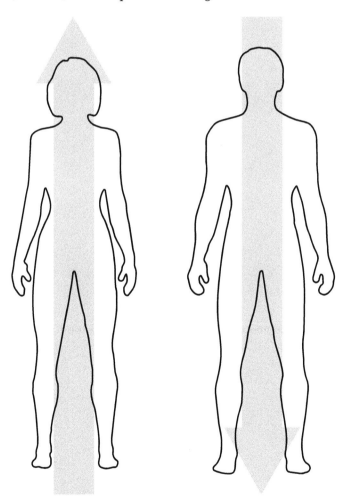

Energetic polarities

In polarity magic, the same principle applies, though here again individual variation has to be taken into account. Most men, though not all, find it easier to work with descending forces, whether these involve bringing the solar current down to earth or channeling the telluric current back to its source. Most women, though not all, similarly find it easier to work with ascending forces, whether these involve bringing the telluric current up into the light or channeling the solar current back to its source. Both the general principle and the existence of individual variations need to be kept in mind as theory spills over into practice.

CHAPTER 4

Polarity in the microcosm

Each individual human being, according to occult philosophy, is a microcosm, a "little universe" in which all the forces of the macrocosm are reflected. It is because each of us contain the macrocosmic forces in miniature, and can align the forces in us with the forces in the cosmos, that we are capable of learning and practicing magic. Just as an athlete needs to know something about the structure and function of his or her material body in order to accomplish feats of strength and skill, in turn, the operative mage needs to know something about the structure and function of the rest of his or her human microcosm in order to accomplish feats of magic.

This involves certain complexities. Like the material body, the subtle bodies of one human being have the same basic structures and functions as the subtle bodies of others, but there are differences—and some of these are extremely important. Polarity work is one of the fields in which these differences cannot be ignored. Just as no one can father a child unless his material body produces viable sperm, and no one can bear a child unless her material body has a uterus that can bring the child to term, the processes of polarity magic require certain structures to be present in the etheric and astral bodies of the participants. These processes also require certain interactions to take place between the participants, which also depend on conditions in the subtle bodies. Abstract as the following teachings may seem, in other words, they have crucial implications for the practical work given in this book.

The subtle bodies

Just as the world consists of more than one plane of existence, occult philosophy teaches that each human being has more than one body. The material body of flesh and blood is only the densest and most obvious of the bodies we all have. Two other bodies, the etheric body or body of life force, and the astral body or body of imagination, occupy the same space as the material body but function on their own planes of being. Then there is the mental sheath, which is in the process of becoming a body but has not accomplished that yet in most human beings. It is when a soul in animal incarnation develops the first traces of a mental sheath that it reincarnates as a human being, or as one of the handful of other animal forms (such as porpoises) that can host the same level of consciousness. It is when the mental sheath becomes a mental body that the soul finishes its pilgrimage through material incarnation, leaves behind the wheel of life and death, and goes on to further potentials for spiritual evolution.

It's important not to make the mistake of thinking of the subtle bodies as mysterious, uncanny, and distant from ordinary life and experience. Every time you get a gut feeling or draw in a deep breath before lifting something heavy, whether you know it or not, you are using your etheric body. Every time you daydream, imagine, or call a memory back to mind, you are using your astral body. Every time you understand the meaning of something, you are putting your mental sheath to work, and helping to transform it into a mental body. These are everyday realities, and your task in learning about your bodies is simply to understand what you have been doing and perceiving all along.

The material body need not be described here. Any good book on human anatomy will teach you as much as you might want to know about it. The etheric body is shaped exactly like the material body but extends a half inch or so beyond the outer surface of the skin. It has its own organs, in the form of energy centers, and its own equivalent of the circulatory system, in the meridians or energy channels that acupuncturists use for healing purposes. Just as the material body receives the substances it needs from food and drink, the etheric body takes in the substances it needs: the lighter or subtler ethers by breathing, the heavier or denser ethers by absorbing the etheric substance found in natural, minimally processed foods. (The starved, unsatisfied feeling many people get when they eat a diet too high in processed foods is a common sign that their etheric bodies are not being properly nourished).

The astral body extends further out than the etheric body, filling a roughly egg-shaped region that extends between eighteen inches and three feet from the outside of the material body; the portion of it outside the material body is what many psychics call the aura. It also has its own organs, in the form of energy centers, but it does not need channels of circulation, because astral substance is constantly flowing at great speed all through the astral body. A particle of astral substance that is beneath your feet at one moment may be above your head a few moments later, or inside your belly, or anywhere else in your astral body. Its energy centers look like vortices or whirlpools when seen by clairvoyant sight.

The mental sheath, finally, is a sphere that surrounds and penetrates the astral, etheric, and material bodies. In most people its outer boundary is indistinct, and it has not yet developed organs or energy centers. The further along the path of spiritual evolution a person has gone, the more definite the outer edge of the mental sheath becomes, and the first rudimentary organs begin to take shape in the mental body as the human stage of evolution reaches its completion. Since the degree of development of the mental sheath varies so significantly from one person to another, the mental sheath has only a limited role in polarity magic, and in most other forms of magic worked by more than one person. It comes into its own in meditation, contemplation, and prayer, the basic disciplines of mysticism.

The accompanying table may help readers sort out the subtle bodies. The Cabalistic, earlier and later Theosophical, and Rosicrucian[17] names for the bodies have been included, so that practitioners of other forms of occultism will have no difficulty making sense of the material in this book.

---

[17] There are many branches of the Rosicrucian movement and not all of them use the same terminology. I have used the terms shared by the Rosicrucian Fellowship and the Societas Rosicruciana in America (SRIA), two branches of the movement whose books are widely available.

	Material Body	Etheric Body	Astral Body	Mental Sheath
Cabala	Guph	Nephesh	Ruach	Neshamah
Theosophy (early)	Sthula Sharira	Linga Sharira	Kama-Manas	Manas
Theosophy (later)	Physical body	Etheric double	Astral body	Mental body
Rosicrucian	Dense body	Vital body	Desire body	Concrete mind

Polarity and the planes

One of the reasons that occult philosophy uses the metaphor of energy when talking about the flow of influences on the higher planes is that these influences behave like electric charges. Anyone who has stroked a longhaired cat in cold dry weather and then touched something made of metal knows how an electric charge can build up and then discharge in a spark. The same thing happens with erotic energies, and with the substance of each of the higher planes more generally: energy, or something that feels very much like energy, builds and then discharges in some suitable direction.

This much is a common human experience. Most of us have felt the buildup of erotic charge during sexual arousal, and many of us have similar experiences in other aspects of human life. To make sense of the way these cycles of charge and discharge play out in polarity magic, it's important to realize that each of the bodies discussed in the previous section of this chapter can build up, discharge, and receive energy from another body of the same plane.

When two people interact, in other words, their material bodies are only two of eight bodies that can be involved. Consider an ordinary hug between two people who aren't sexually attracted to each other. The material bodies of the people involved are the least important aspects of the embrace, and if only these two bodies are involved, the hug feels cold and unpleasant. If the two people in question are compatible in certain ways—a point that will be explored in detail a little further on—contact between the etheric bodies brings a sense of well-being. Contact between the astral bodies provides emotional comfort, and contact between the mental sheaths often gives intuitive perceptions of the other person's state of mind. If the mental sheaths of both people are sufficiently developed and attuned to each other, close contact can lead to telepathic experiences.

Sex follows similar principles. If only the material bodies are involved, sex is little more than friction, and tends to be emotionally and even physically unsatisfying. When the etheric bodies are involved, the life force flows freely and sex becomes a healing and vivifying experience. When the astral bodies are involved, the emotions come into play, and when the mental sheaths are involved, sex can become a profoundly transformative experience. All these except the first are also possible outside of any form of physical sexual contact.

These interactions are not always easy, and may not even be possible, between certain individuals. The reason for this is that subtle bodies, like material bodies, differ in polarity, and the flow of subtle energies from person to person depends on having compatible polarities on the subtle planes. To understand how this works in practice, we can begin with a simple example, an energetic interaction—with or without sexual contact—between a woman and a man who have the most common polarization of their subtle bodies.

	Most Women	Most Men
Mental plane:	masculine/active	feminine/receptive
Astral plane:	feminine/receptive	masculine/active
Etheric plane:	masculine/active	feminine/receptive
Material plane:	feminine/receptive	masculine/active

It's important to keep in mind that these categorizations are relative, not absolute. They are not fixed rules, but simply outline the usual pattern under ordinary conditions. Most women, though by no means all, tend more often than not to build up a charge of energy on the mental and etheric planes; most men, but by no means all, tend more often than not to build up a charge of energy on the astral and material planes. When a man and a woman in these states have sexual contact, the exchange of energy moves from active to receptive on each plane.

This can be understood best by seeing how the process works on the material plane. On that plane, the female body is adapted for one role in reproduction—the role of receiving semen from the male, using it to fertilize an ovum, and nurturing the fertilized ovum in the womb as it becomes a child and prepares for an independent life. The male body is adapted for the corresponding role of providing the semen that sets the process in motion. The two in combination make something possible that one alone cannot do.

One of the basic concepts of occult polarity theory is that this same pattern is true on the other planes of being that humans can experience. Notice, however, that in the example we're considering, the flow goes in alternating directions on different planes. In most cases, due to the differing polarities of male and female subtle bodies, a surplus of etheric energy tends to flow from the woman to the man. In most astral interactions, the flow is from the man to the woman, and in most mental interactions, it runs from the woman to the man. In the case of the subtle bodies, as already noted, these are general predispositions rather than hard and fast rules, but these patterns are common enough that they can be treated as a good basic outline.

Masturbation provides a useful example of how this works in practice. Most men, if they masturbate a great deal, end up feeling weak and drained. Most women, if they do the same thing, end up feeling clogged and congested. This difference makes perfect sense from the perspective of polarity. Most of the time, in heterosexual intercourse, the life force—the substance of the etheric plane—flows from the woman into the man. Because human genitals have become specialized for reproduction through long ages of evolution, genital masturbation makes the body prepare for intercourse in the same way that thinking of slicing a lemon makes the mouth water. If there is no female partner to provide him with etheric energy, however, the man who masturbates feels weak, because his etheric body expects an inflow of energy it does not receive. If there is no male partner to draw out and receive her etheric energy, the woman who masturbates feels clogged, because her etheric body builds up a charge of etheric energy that has nowhere to go.

Apply the same principle to the next plane up, the astral plane, and the relationship usually works in reverse. One good example is "fanfic"—the kind of amateur fiction, very popular on the internet as I write this, that takes some existing set of characters and settings from media and spins stories about them. Fanfic is mostly written by women. That happens because most women have female astral bodies, and so their imaginations work best when fertilized with images and ideas from some outside source. The male imagination is less dependent on outside stimulus. It needs expression, not fertilization.

On the mental plane, in turn, things work the other way around. It's legendary how often male artists, writers, musicians, and other creators need female companionship in order to create. They don't receive ideas or imagery from the women in their lives. Instead, the experience of sexual and romantic desire makes it possible for them to create. Female artists, by contrast, rarely have a comparable need. Why? Most men have female mental sheaths, which need fertilization. Most women have male mental sheaths, and so they need to inspire rather than to be inspired.

Variations in polarity

While the arrangement of polarities given above is the most common, a significant minority of men and women have a different arrangement. The etheric body is almost always the reverse polarity of the material body, but in something like ten per cent of the population, the higher bodies have a reversed polarization, as shown in the accompanying table.

	Some Women	Some Men
Mental plane:	feminine/receptive	masculine/active
Astral plane:	masculine/active	feminine/receptive
Etheric plane:	masculine/active	feminine/receptive
Material plane:	feminine/receptive	masculine/active

People with this alternate polarity arrangement tend to have creative lives that follow patterns more common in the other sex. This is where, among other things, you find men who write fanfic and women who need to be in love in order to stimulate their creative processes. Very often such people have a difficult time with romantic heterosexual relationships unless they can find a partner who also has the alternate polarization. There are also other, less common arrangements—for example, it very occasionally happens that someone is one sex on the material plane and the other sex on all three of the subtle planes. This also tends to be associated with relationship troubles—again, unless a partner with the matching polarization can be found.

This same consideration can be extended more broadly. As noted earlier, the basic modes of polarization just discussed are very broad generalizations, not rigid laws. Even in a relationship between a man and a woman who have the usual polarizations, it happens sometimes that the current of etheric force goes from the man to the woman, the current of astral influence goes from the woman to the man, and the current of mental influence goes from the man to the woman. This happens because at that time, the man has a stronger charge of etheric energy, the woman a stronger charge of astral energy, and so on. Whichever body on each plane has the stronger charge at the moment of interaction will tend to release energy into the corresponding body with a weaker charge.

This has to be understood to make sense of the occult energetics of gay and lesbian relationships. Between any two people of the same sex, one will usually have a more strongly energized etheric body, and the life force will flow from that person to the other during energy exchange. In the same way, one of them will usually have a more strongly charged astral or mental body, and astral or mental energy will flow from that person to the other. Sometimes these energy flows will reverse with changes in the relative charge of the subtle bodies, but this also happens with heterosexual couples.

The main thing to keep in mind with gay and lesbian couples is that the flow of energy is less easy to predict than with heterosexual couples. Far more often than not, a man and a woman working in polarity will have the first pattern of energy flow described earlier—an etheric flow from woman to man and an astral flow from man to woman—but there is no standard pattern for two men or two women working in polarity. The same lack of a standard pattern is often true for intersex people as well. As always, each case needs to be judged individually.

There are also variations in polarity that come with age, and these have roles of their own to play in human interaction. Until they reach the age of seven, children do not yet have fully independent etheric bodies, and from then until puberty their etheric bodies are still ripening. During these years they need nonsexual contact with the etheric bodies of adults in order to thrive. This is why very young children in old-fashioned orphanages who received very little human contact so often weakened and died, even if they received adequate food and the other material necessities of life. Etheric starvation was very often the cause of death, though "failure to thrive" was usually what went on the certificate. The child who runs up to Grandma to ask for a hug is receiving something essential to its well-being.

Puberty brings a dramatic shift. Most young people during puberty, boys as well as girls, have abundant etheric energy, though girls typically have more than boys. The peak intensity of life force is reached around the point of full reproductive maturity and then declines with age. The powerful sexual attraction many straight and gay men alike feel for younger partners is rooted in part in this energetic process, since most men need to absorb etheric energy during sexual interactions, and younger partners of either sex have it in abundance. Yes, some women also feel this kind of attraction to young partners, especially those women who have reached middle age and whose etheric bodies are no longer as full of the life force as they once were.

The astral body follows a similar trajectory, but at a later age. The astral body becomes independent around the age of fourteen, around the time the etheric body finishes ripening, and does not reach its full power until around the age of twenty-eight. Before this happens the astral body remains highly permeable to emotional patterns from others, which helps explain the potent role of peer pressure and fashion-consciousness in the lives of teens.

After the astral body has finished maturing, the mental sheath becomes independent, though the process of ripening and maturing the mental sheath takes many lives and so only a small part of the work can be done in any one life. The very old, if they have worked on its development, often have a mental sheath at the peak of its powers even after the astral, etheric, and physical bodies have weakened considerably.

All these points can be summed up straightforwardly enough. People's subtle bodies differ just as much as their material bodies: this is the rule to keep in mind. These divergences are important factors to consider in preparing for polarity magic.

The role of imagination

While the most powerful currents of erotic energy flow on the etheric plane, the astral plane is the level of being on which most of the work of ceremonial magic takes place. There are complex reasons for this habit, some of them historical in nature, but the astral plane is also easy for most people to contact, experience, and work with. As mentioned in the previous chapter, we all experience the astral plane every night in our dreams, whether we remember them or not. We also work with the astral plane every time we think, daydream, remember—and especially every time we use our imaginations.

Giordano Bruno, the Renaissance mage discussed in an earlier chapter, taught that the core motive power of magic is erotic attraction roused and directed by the imagination.[18] This approach draws on a common human experience. Most people know what it is like to daydream or fantasize about an erotic image or situation, and have this act of the imagination result in sexual arousal. Bruno used this approach to empower the images that were central to his magical practice. Such images, formulated in the mind or expressed outwardly in forms such as painting and sculpture, were central to many forms of Renaissance magic.

It was for this reason that John Calvin and other theologians of the era that followed rejected the imagination altogether as evil—some Puritan writers argued, in fact, that the Biblical commandment against making graven images should be extended to the imagination, so that imagining anything at all was a sin. The ideology of scientific materialism that took over from Reformation Protestant thought to create the modern world inherited the same distrust of the human imagination, but expressed it differently. From the viewpoint of the scientific materialist, the imagination is not evil but simply false, portraying things that don't exist. It's for this reason that many people use the word "imaginary" to mean "unreal."

From the point of view of occultism, by contrast, the world experienced by imagination is a real world. It is not the same as the world experienced by the senses—again, the planes are discrete and not continuous—but the astral plane, the plane that imagination perceives and shapes, is not simply limited to the inside of any one person's head. Since most of us have very little experience using our imaginations, we are in the position of an infant who has very little experience using its hands and feet. This is why most people experience the astral plane, the realm of the imagination, as a jumble of disconnected images. Just as infants must learn to reach with their hands, feel things with their fingers, and eventually get up and walk on their feet, novice ceremonial mages must learn to attend to what the imagination shows them, and

---

[18] Bruno's most important works on the subject, *De Magia* (*On Magic*) and *De Vinculis in Genere* (*On Linkages in General*), are difficult to find in English translation, but their contents are well summarized in Culianu 1987.

when this is appropriate, to set aside the imaginative experiences generated by their own minds so that they can encounter the landscape of the astral plane.

The French philosopher and historian Henry Corbin pointed out in an influential essay, *Mundus Imaginalis*, that the imagination under the right circumstances can encounter things that are as objectively real as the material world.[19] He proposed the term "imaginal" as a substitute for the dismissive label "imaginary," and spoke of the *mundus imaginalis* or imaginal world as the realm, well known to mystics and mages alike, where things experienced by the imagination are concrete realities. This is a useful concept and of course it fits closely with the traditions of ceremonial magic.

The constructive use of the imagination, in turn, is one of the things that gives ceremonial magic its power. When any image is built up in the imagination by two or more people, it becomes a reality on the astral plane. The more often it is constructed and the more attention and effort goes into making it, the more stable it becomes, and the easier it is for the influences of other planes to flow along it. In the practical work of polarity magic, the imagination is used constantly. One of its principal uses is to create channels through which erotic energy can flow from person to person, and from the working to the target of the magic.

It is important to treat these channels as concrete realities on their own plane, to build them up as precisely as you would put together pipes for water, and to dissolve them once you have finished the work. Remembering the reality of the imaginal world or, as ceremonial mages call it, the astral plane is one way to help yourself keep this in mind.

Vertical polarity

The channels just described can extend from plane to plane as well as from person to person. This flexibility is crucial to the work ahead. In the discussion of polarity forces earlier in this chapter I have treated the process of charge and discharge between the subtle bodies as though each body is isolated from the others. This is a helpful first approximation, because energy flows on the same plane are more

---

[19] Corbin 1976.

reliable than those that move from plane to plane. In polarity magic, however, and in many other expressions of erotic energy, flows that pass from plane to plane play a very important role.

In a very real sense, the relationship of your bodies among themselves is a polarity relationship. If, like most people, your bodies have alternating polarities, the descent of creative force through your bodies works in a way not too different from the way that energy flows from person to person in a polarity relationship. Your mental sheath, which receives energy from the spiritual planes, polarizes with your astral body and charges it. The surplus energy on the astral then polarizes with your etheric body and charges it, and your etheric body does the same thing and charges your material body. This is shown symbolically in the accompanying diagram.

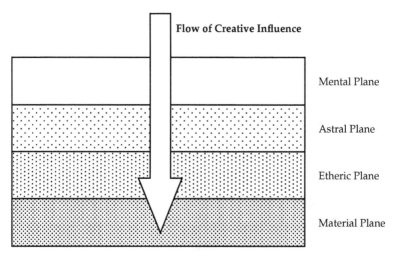

The descending current

In the course of reproductive sex, this descent of force is paired with another, ascending current. When a child is conceived in the ordinary way, energy flows down into manifestation through the bodies of the father-to-be, passes into the material body of the mother-to-be, and rises back up out of manifestation through her bodies. It is of course possible for a child to be conceived without the involvement of this pattern of energies—for example, by means of artificial insemination—but a child conceived with the help of the descending and ascending energy flow will benefit from it physically and mentally, especially in early childhood.

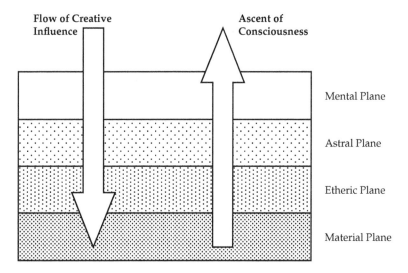

The two currents

These vertical polarities are also of practical importance in polarity magic. In most cases, as noted earlier, the descending current of energy flows most easily through men, and the ascending current flows most easily through women. This can be put to practical use in workings where the primary polarity flow is between a man and a woman; this is especially useful when the solar and telluric currents are involved in the work. In same-sex polarity pairings, or workings that involve one or more intersex people, it can require careful experimentation to work out which person is best suited to bring through any given current of energy.

Horizontal polarity

The term "horizontal polarity" inevitably fields its share of wry jokes, but it makes a useful label for a second mode of energy flow in polarity magic. The vertical currents described above must pass from one part-ner to the other by way of one or more of the levels of being, and this process normally sets a circular flow in motion between the partners. This horizontal circuit is crucial in polarity workings; it can take place in at least three ways: the circuit of conception, the polarity magic circuit, and the devotional mysticism circuit.

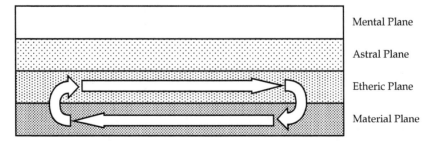

Circuit of conception

The most material of these is shown in the diagram of the circuit of conception. In reproductive sex, the flow of etheric energy and the flow of physical substance form a circuit of force which reaches its peak at orgasm. When this circuit is complete and energy flows freely through it, the sexual act is most likely to result in the conception of a child.

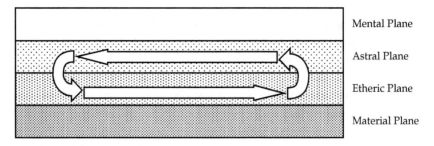

Polarity magic circuit

Polarity magic works with a different circuit. Here the two planes that play the most important roles are the etheric and astral planes, and the physical plane is not directly involved in the process. Here etheric force flows one way and astral force flows the other. The circuit they form is less focused on a specific moment such as orgasm, and can therefore be maintained at high intensity for the duration of a magical working.

A third circuit is worth considering here, though it very rarely plays a role in polarity magic. This is a circuit on the astral and mental planes, which is central to devotional mysticism. Here the flow goes one way on the mental plane and the other way on the astral plane. Under most situations it can only be done if one partner is fully awake on the mental plane, which is why it generally takes place between a human being and a deity, or under some circumstances between an ordinary human being and a saint, sage, or adept. Its relevance here is simply that it shows how the pattern already discussed can function on yet another pair of planes.

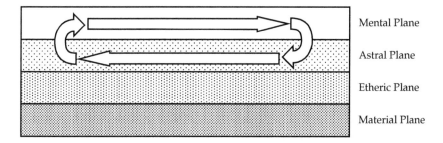

Mental Plane

Astral Plane

Etheric Plane

Material Plane

Devotional mysticism circuit

These circuits of force show, among other things, the practical application of the way that different bodies have different polarities, as discussed in the previous chapter. Energy on any given plane flows from a masculine body to a feminine body. If your astral body is male and your etheric body is female—as already noted, this is the case with most men—you will get the best results in polarity magic if you work with someone whose astral body is female and whose etheric body is male—the most common arrangement among women.

What happens if two men with the usual arrangement of bodies set out to do polarity work together? It depends partly on their sexual orientation and partly on the relative strength of their etheric and astral bodies. If they are both attracted to men, one has a stronger astral body, and the other has a stronger etheric body, the polarity magic circuit shown above can flow freely, and polarity magic is possible. If one or both of them don't find men erotically attractive, or if one of them is stronger than the other on both planes, nothing will happen. When two women with the usual arrangement of bodies set out to work polarity magic, the same principles apply.

Matters become more complex when one partner has the usual arrangement of plane polarities and the other has an alternate arrangement.

Consider a polarity working between a woman who has the usual arrangement and a man who has the two higher bodies reversed— a feminine astral body and a masculine mental body, just like his partner. In this case there will be a normal etheric flow from the woman to the man, but the astral flow back from the man to the woman is a more complex matter. He will have to make a sustained effort to strengthen his astral body so that the return flow can take place on that plane, or the energy will tend to default downward to the material plane, resulting in ordinary sexual arousal.

If a man with the ordinary arrangement of bodies does polarity work with a woman with the higher bodies reversed, by contrast, the difficulty is that both partners have masculine astral bodies, and this prevents the return flow on the astral plane just as effectively. In this case the woman will have to make a sustained effort to render her astral body receptive during the working, so that the flow will take place on that plane, instead of being diverted to the material genitals and ordinary sexual arousal.

Other combinations are possible, of course, and in fact they are encountered tolerably often in polarity work. It is important for anybody who is considering the practice of polarity magic to get some sense of the way their subtle bodies polarize, and to discuss this with potential partners in polarity work. Since the polarities of the subtle bodies are general tendencies, not rigid laws, it's usually possible for two people who find each other erotically and emotionally attractive to do polarity magic together—in fact, the existence of the attraction is a good sign that the energy will flow as needed. Even so, it's best for everyone involved to know what issues might be involved in the practice. Chapter 5 will offer certain guidelines for this, but individual factors always take precedence in this work. A sustained effort from all participants to communicate clearly and gently about these very sensitive issues is important, and should be cultivated by people working with polarity magic.

Subtle energy centers

Occult traditions around the world include teachings about energy centers, which have the same functions in the subtle bodies that physical organs have in the material body. Many people these days have heard of the seven chakras, a set of invisible focal points of energy located along the midline of the body from the base of the spine to the crown of the head. This is one example of a system of energy centers—but it is far from the only one.

There is a great deal of seeming disagreement among different traditions when it comes to the location and function of these centers. The divergence is more apparent than real. Esoteric teachings in various parts of the world have identified some 360 energy centers in the human body, and each system of occult training chooses a handful of these to develop. The choice of centers reflects the fine details of the system of training, since each center has its own distinct effects on the subtle bodies when it is awakened.

The subtle side of erotic activity normally functions through four principal energy centers. The first of these is the genital center, which is located just above the base of the penis or the clitoris, a little inside the physical body. The second is the throat center, which is located just behind the notch in the collarbone where the throat meets the upper chest. The third and fourth are the palm centers, which are located at the base of each palm, just above the first line of each wrist. It is no accident that most forms of lovemaking involve contact between the parts of the material body that are close to, and linked energetically with, these centers: that is to say, the genital region, the lips, and the hands.

Of these centers the throat and genital centers are primary, and the palm centers are secondary. It is no accident, in other words, that the two primary centers are included in the standard energy center systems used in Western occultism. The system of seven chakras includes a great many variations, but most versions used by occultists in the West include the genital or Svadhishthana chakra and the throat or Vishuddhi chakra. The Middle Pillar exercise, the most widely used system of energy work in Western occultism not based on the chakras, places its Yesod center at the genitals and its Daath center at the throat. The same centers also play a role in the very different system of seven vortices used in some American Rosicrucian orders.[20] (One implication of this is that all these exercises can be used as preparation for polarity work.)

The way that these centers and their associated body parts traditionally served as a marker of closeness in ordinary relationships reflects the varying intensities with which erotic energies flow through them. When my generation was young, certainly, it still meant something

---

[20] For more on these energy centers, see respectively Motoyama 1981, Regardie 1945, and Greer 2023c.

when a couple began holding hands, but that was still a tentative mode of contact. Kissing took the relationship to another level, and of course any contact with the genital area took it as far as it could go short of the enduring magical link formed in traditional marriage ceremonies.

In the same way, the palm centers are used in the polarity workings in this book to establish the initial contact between the subtle bodies of the participants, and centers aligned with the body core are brought into play later on. The genital and throat centers are not used directly, however. Instead, a different center in the midline of the body—the solar plexus center—is the point of energetic contact between the participants in the core stages of the workings, once initial contact has been made through the palm centers. The solar plexus center is located just below the ribcage and behind the stomach, roughly halfway between the navel and the heart.

The energy center takes its name from the solar plexus itself, a mass of nerve tissue about the size of a cat's brain, which manages the vital organs of the body and also serves as a focus of the unconscious mind. Many kinds of psychic perception function through this center; so do ordinary "gut feelings," which are the simplest form of psychic awareness. The center's connection to psychism makes it especially useful in polarity magic. Some traditional occult schools teach exercises to loosen the muscles of the solar plexus region and increase blood flow to the plexus itself. One of these is included in the next chapter, and regular practice of this exercise will give your polarity workings improved results.

There are two good reasons why the solar plexus center is used in the methods of polarity magic given in this book. First, working directly with the genital centers makes the sublimation of erotic energy more difficult than it has to be, since anything that stimulates the genital center directs the life force into physical arousal. Letting the energies rise to the level of the solar plexus makes it easier to redirect them into the work of magic.

The second reason is a little subtler. The throat and genital centers, as mentioned above, normally have opposite polarities. The genital center usually has the same polarity as the etheric body as a whole, and the throat center has the opposite polarity—in most cases, the polarity of the astral body. In reproductive heterosexual intercourse, these patterns of polarization encourage the circuit of conception to be formed, resulting in sexual arousal, intercourse, and (where possible) pregnancy and eventual childbirth. This is entirely appropriate in its place, but polarity magic requires erotic energies to be directed elsewhere, and so stimulation of these two centers is not helpful.

The process of sublimation, rather, is facilitated by using the energy center at the solar plexus. Placed halfway between these two centers, the solar plexus center is in a state of balance, and can give and receive energy as needed. Since the flow of energy in a polarity working will vary depending on a galaxy of variables affecting the participants, working through the solar plexus allows the energies to ebb and flow freely as needed.

The solar plexus is therefore the main center used in most of the workings that follow. One sequence of workings, however, also activates the third eye center, which is located inside the front of the head, behind the flat space between the eyebrows. The energies of the throat center can be redirected to the third eye center in the same way that the energies of the genital center are raised up to the solar plexus center. Activating the third eye center is an effective way to awaken clairvoyant and visionary perceptions, and workings of the type just indicated are intended to accomplish that. The scrying ritual given in Chapter 6 is an example of the way this can be used to open the third eye center and develop the skills of seership; other rituals of the same kind can be devised by polarity mages once the basic techniques have been mastered.

CHAPTER 5

Preparing for polarity magic

T he theoretical material discussed in the last two chapters must be studied carefully and understood in order for polarity magic to be practiced with good results. Theoretical knowledge, however, is not the only kind of preparation needed for polarity workings. Certain magical skills, some elementary and others much less so, also need to be learned and mastered so that polarity workings can be performed with effect. Certain specific exercises must be learned and practiced regularly so that you can use the specific ritual and energetic forms taught in this book, and some wholly practical steps also need to be taken to prepare for the work ahead.

The most important requirement for polarity workings, as already mentioned, is a solid practical background in some system of ceremonial magic. Polarity magic is not for beginners. It requires the mastery of the standard skills of ceremonial magic. It therefore cannot be done effectively by people whose only experience in magical practice consists of casting the occasional spell lifted out of a book or downloaded from a website, taking in the occasional weekend workshop, or attending community full moon ceremonies or sabbat celebrations of the kind that are open to the general public.

There is nothing wrong with this level of magical practice, if that happens to be what works for you. There are many ways to practice magic and many levels of involvement in the magical path. Not everyone can or should invest the same sort of time, effort and passion in their magic that a classical musician puts into their music and instrument. That said, so long as you stay at the level just outlined, there will be kinds of magic you will never be skilled enough to do. Just as it takes rigorous training and daily practice to learn how to play music by Bach, it takes equally rigorous training and the same degree of daily effort to be able to practice the more complex forms of ceremonial magic. It really is as simple as that.

How can you judge whether you have the necessary training and experience to take up polarity magic? The simplest way is to read the next two chapters, and see if any practice mentioned there is unfamiliar to you. If so, you know what you have to learn in order to get ready for the work ahead, and the necessary knowledge can be found in hundreds of books currently in print; all you need to do is get one or more of them, and start practicing. If you have no trouble figuring out how to do everything the workings in this book require, on the other hand, you are ready to proceed.

Your first step beyond these initial requirements is to expand your current magical work by adding a set of basic exercises relevant to polarity magic. The first exercise is a simple visualization and meditation practice intended to develop your awareness of sexual energies. It can be adapted to fit whatever form of meditation you currently practice as part of your daily magical practices.

The second exercise is designed to energize and clear the solar plexus center, the most important energy center used in the ceremonies given in this book. It was once standard practice in occult schools all over the Western world; it has been neglected by some more recently founded traditions, but it is worth bringing back into common use.

The third exercise will provide you with the symbolic tools needed to awaken and direct subtle energies through your palm centers, which as noted in Chapter 4 are used in the ceremonies ahead. This practice is specific to the system of magic, healing, and occult spirituality I was taught by my late teacher John Gilbert, but it can be used with good effect in any system of ceremonial magic.

Experiencing polarity

The trained imagination is a central tool of ceremonial magic. Most of the workings given in this book rely on it. In order to make the best use of them, you will need to develop a clear imaginative sense of the nature and feeling of masculine and feminine erotic energies, so that you can use appropriate imagery to direct those energies in magic.

Here again, please note: masculine and feminine *energies*, not persons. Every human being was conceived through the interaction of masculine and feminine principles, and we all carry both masculine and feminine energies within ourselves, manifesting each of them in one or more of our bodies. Your task in this exercise is to differentiate them clearly so that you can work with them in practice. These are the power sources of polarity magic, so if you can't or won't do this, polarity magic of the kind taught in this book is closed to you.

Most people find it easiest to start with the sex to which they feel the strongest erotic attraction. Work with the energies of that sex in your first session, then with the opposite sex in the next session. Continue to alternate until you can call up either sexual energy at will. The exercise is performed as follows:

First, enter into meditation in any way you prefer.

Second, imagine a sphere of light in front of you. It is eighteen inches to two feet across, and it hovers in the air a few feet away from you. The color of the light is yours to choose; let it be a color that represents one sex to you. For example, if you happen to be traditionally minded, make it blue if you are going to work with masculine energies, or pink if you are going to work with feminine energies. If some other pair of colors works better for you, use those instead.

Third, imagine the sphere of light filling with erotic energies. If the sphere represents the sex to which you feel the most erotic attraction, remember how persons of that sex felt to you in your own erotic encounters, and imagine that feeling as being present in the sphere. If you are heterosexual and the sphere represents your own sex, remember how you felt in those erotic encounters, and imagine that feeling in the sphere. Gay and lesbian polarity mages sometimes have trouble making use of the labels "masculine" and "feminine;" in this case it's often better to think of the two energy patterns as active and receptive. Every person who has sexual feelings has experienced both these energies at one time or another; draw on your own experiences of active and receptive sexual energy, and let that guide you in building the imagined charge.

Fourth, allow the charge of erotic energy in the sphere to dissipate. You may find it easiest to do this by letting the energies follow the flow of vertical polarity: that is, if you have generated masculine energy, allow it to descend to the center of the earth; if feminine energy, allow it to rise up to the sun or the stars. In either case, take your time and allow the energy to dissipate completely before you close the meditation.

This exercise should be done daily until you can easily imagine and perceive both energies. At that point, it should be replaced by the exercise to awaken the palm centers, which is given below.

Solar plexus exercise

The solar plexus is the most important energy center in the subtle body. It is also the main center of the sympathetic nervous system, the network of nerves that manage the vital organs and also the genitals, largely independent of the brain. As explained in the previous chapter, it is the energy center through which most of the erotic energies flow in the workings given in this book. The ability to allow energies to flow into or out of the solar plexus is essential to these workings, and the extent to which you can do this will determine how much success you will have in polarity magic.

Fortunately, there are effective ways to clear away blockages and improve the flow of energy through this center. Muscular tension in the region around the solar plexus interferes with the flow of subtle energy and the free activity of the sympathetic nervous system. A simple exercise will relax the muscles around the solar plexus and make the practical work of this book easier and more effective. It is done in the following way:

First, sit in a comfortable chair or sofa, or lie face up on a bed. Take a few moments to relax as much as you can. Then draw in a deep breath and push out your stomach as you do so. This allows you to draw the air down into the very bottom of your lungs.

Second, without breathing out, suck your belly in and push your chest out, moving the air from the lower to the upper part of your lungs. Push your belly out again and let your chest fall, sending the air back down.

Do this twice more, so that you've sent the air from the lower lungs to the upper lungs and back again, without breathing out. Then, finally, let the breath out. Let yourself go completely limp, and breathe slowly and comfortably for a little while.

Third, repeat the same sequence—breathing in, sending the air up and back three times, and breathing out—twice more, so you have done the whole sequence three times, relaxing and breathing easily between each sequence. (When you can do this easily three times, you can increase the number of repetitions.)

Fourth, when you have finished, draw in and let out three slow gentle breaths. As you do so, turn your attention to your solar plexus: the center of your subjective mind, the mass of nerve tissue just below your ribcage and just behind your stomach. Imagine it shining warm and golden, like a little sun inside you. Feel the golden light spreading all through your body. When you have finished the three breaths, let go of the image and go about the rest of your day.

This exercise should be done every day, and is best done every morning before your first meal. Go easy on yourself at first—unless you're in good physical shape, the muscles in your abdomen may not be used to the effort, and can be overstrained.

Awakening the palm centers

The palm centers also play an important role in the work ahead, and need to be charged with energy. It sometimes happens that these centers are blocked by tension in the same way as the solar plexus. To check the state of your palm centers, try using the thumb of each hand to rub all over the palm in small circles, pressing moderately hard. If you feel pain or stiffness in your palm, you might benefit from repeating this daily.

Whether or not you need this, a simple ritual method for opening and activating the palm centers is a necessary part of the work ahead. Energy contact through these centers is the first stage in each of the polarity workings given in this book. The method given here has a great many other uses; I was first introduced to it as part of a system of energy healing, which I have published elsewhere in two versions.[21]

---

[21] See Greer 2020 and Greer 2023b.

It is probably necessary to clarify one point before we proceed. In this exercise, feminine energies are assigned to the left hand, and masculine energies to the right hand. This does not mean that the left side of your body is naturally more feminine and the right side more masculine, or anything of that kind. It is simply necessary to differentiate the two energies within the body, in a way that allows you to make energy contact with another trained person.

In the two-person form of polarity working, you will be seated facing your partner. If you both raise your palms facing each other, your right hand will be facing your partner's left hand, and your left hand will be facing your partner's right hand. This brings active, masculine energies into interaction with the receptive, feminine energies and permits the free energy flow that makes polarity magic work.

Similarly, in the four-person form, you and the three other participants will be seated on the four sides of a square. If all four of you raise your palms, angled outward to face the two people closest to you, once again each of you will have your right hand facing another person's left hand and your left hand facing another person's right hand. This allows the same free flow of energies as before. This only works, however, if all participants have charged their palms in the same way. Here as elsewhere, there's a point to doing things the traditional way even if that way involves certain arbitrary choices.

With that said, we can proceed. The basic procedure is as follows:

First: sit with your feet side by side and your knees touching each other, or as close to this as the shape of your body will permit you to do comfortably. Place your hands palms down on your thighs. Your back should be reasonably straight but not stiff, and your head balanced easily on your neck. (Statues of enthroned Egyptian gods and goddesses are good guides to this posture.) Spend a few minutes breathing slowly and smoothly, while relaxing every muscle you do not need to use to support your body in the posture.

Second: turn the palms over. Then, with the index finger of the right hand, trace a triangle on the left palm, as follows: start at the base of the palm, where it joins the wrist; draw a line with your right index finger up to the base of the left index finger, then across to the base of the little finger, then down to the starting point. Imagine as vividly as possible that the lines drawn by your right index finger are traced in intense blue light.

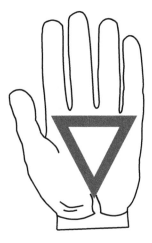

Water triangle

Third: next, starting from the same point and using the same finger, draw a circle around the palm, and then a line from the same point several inches along the forearm. Imagine as vividly as possible that the circle and line you draw with your right index finger are traced in intense green light.

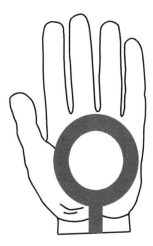

Earth circle

Fourth: now place your right hand back on your right thigh, palm up. With the index finger of the left hand, trace a triangle on the right palm, as follows: start at the point between the bases of the middle and ring fingers of your right hand; draw a line with your left index finger down to the base of your thumb, then across to the opposite side of the heel of your hand, then up to the starting point. Imagine as vividly as possible that the lines drawn by your left index finger are traced in intense red light.

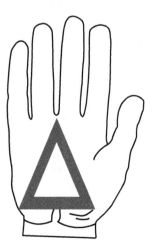

Fire triangle

Fifth: from the same starting point between the bases of the middle and ring fingers of your right hand, trace a circle on your right palm with the index finger of your left hand, and then a line from the same point between the middle and ring fingers to their ends. Imagine as vividly as possible that the lines drawn by your left index finger are traced in intense yellow light.

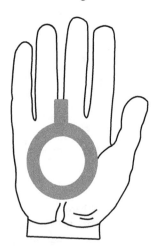

Air circle

Sixth: Now replace your left hand on your left thigh and leave your right hand on your right thigh. Both palms are facing up. Visualize the triangles and circles on both hands in the colors given above. Then imagine your left palm charged with feminine energy and your right palm charged with masculine energy. Allow the work you have done with female and male energies in the first exercise to shape your sense of how these two energies manifest. Spend five minutes or so building up a sense of the feminine force in your left hand and the masculine force in your right hand.

Seventh: raise your hands from your thighs and bring them together at solar plexus level. To do this, hold the right hand with the palm facing left, the thumb side toward your body, and the fingers pointing upwards, and the left hand with the palm facing right, the thumb side up, and the fingers pointing forward, away from your body.

Join the bases of the palms, so that the little hollows at the center of the base of each palm come into contact. The fingers may be straight or slightly curved, depending on your personal preference. Allow the feminine and masculine energies in your palms to flow together through the point of contact. Feel the connection between the energies. Hold this position for several minutes at least.

Eighth: you have three choices at this point.

(a) If you are simply doing this as part of your daily practices, to awaken the flow of polarity energies through yourself, draw the hands apart and rest them palms down on your thighs. Allow the energies you have built up in your palms to flow into your body as a whole. Relax and breathe slowly and smoothly for a few minutes, and then end the practice.

(b) If you are about to do polarity work with another person, proceed directly to the work.

(c) Once you have finished the polarity work, or in any other situation in which you have awakened polarity energies in your palms, close the palm centers by placing your hands together again in the same position described in Step Seven above: left palm facing right, right palm facing left, the fingers of the left hand pointing forward and the fingers of your right hand pointing up. Feel the connection of the energies. When you are ready, raise the fingertips of the left hand while keeping the palms joined at the base, so that the two hands end up parallel to each other, palm to palm and fingers to fingers. Then draw the hands apart and clap them briskly together once to disperse the energy connection. This completes the working.

This practice should be done at least once a day, so that you can awaken the palm centers easily whenever you choose.

Selecting a partner

The preparatory steps just given can be done by yourself. Before you can go any further than this in polarity magic, however, you will need at least one other person to practice with. This is where the most significant difficulties usually come in. Polarity magic requires at least two participants, who feel emotional and erotic attraction to each other but have agreed not to express that attraction in the ordinary way. To say that this isn't always easy to arrange is to understate the matter considerably.

Alongside the obvious problems, it is also the case that when it comes to erotic and romantic relationships, many people aren't honest with their partners, or with themselves, about what they want and what they are willing to offer. Anyone who teaches and practices polarity magic will soon meet people who say they want to get involved in polarity workings, and may actually believe this, but whose actions make it clear that what they actually want is a sexual relationship or an opportunity to act out some stereotyped emotional drama. The neglected spouse whose real purpose is to make his or her mate jealous, the would-be Casanova who hopes to rack up a string of sexual conquests using occultism as a cover story, the person in a failed marriage who doesn't have the courage to walk out on his or her spouse and is hoping to get into a very public love affair that will convince the spouse to walk out instead: these and others like them are familiar sights.

The point of polarity magic, however, is not to increase the supply of melodrama in a world already very well stocked with it! Your task as a polarity mage, rather, is to find a partner with whom you can perform a set of emotionally and spiritually intense workings involving no physical contact at all. That can be a challenge. In some ways, it was easier in Dion Fortune's time, when divorce was legally and socially difficult, and so there were a great many unhappily married people who didn't want to have love affairs but needed something to do with their erotic energies. It was also easier at times when most occultists belonged to magical lodges and occult societies, in which everyone was interested in magic and a few discreet comments could attract the attention of those who might consider polarity work.

Between changes in sexual mores and the decline of the old magical orders and societies, matters are not quite as easy nowadays. Those readers of this book who belong to a magical lodge or an occult organization have certain advantages here, provided that the teachings and leadership of the lodge or organization are comfortable with polarity magic; some lodges, for that matter, may choose to make polarity magic a part of their curriculum, in which case finding partners for the work becomes relatively simple. Those not so fortunate will have to find some other route, which will depend on circumstances.

Older works on magical polarity, very much including those by Dion Fortune, also include a range of other restrictions. These were based partly on the social and sexual customs of the time when they were written and partly on the idiosyncratic personal experiences of the authors. Fortune herself, for example, could not polarize with gay men, and laid it down as a rule in her writings that gay men couldn't practice polarity magic. More recent practitioners have had good reason to amend this, since gay men can certainly work polarity magic with other gay men, and some can polarize effectively with women as well. Some straight women, for example, have a strong attraction to gay men, and some gay men reciprocate that attraction; wry talk in the gay community about "fruit flies" is one measure of this phenomenon. A polarity partnership between a straight woman and a gay man along these lines, should they feel the necessary emotional attraction to each other, can work extremely well.

In general, the presence of mutual erotic and emotional attraction is your best guide to choosing a partner for polarity work, and the absence of any such attraction means that no such working should be attempted. Assuming that because you are attracted to a certain person, that person ought to be attracted to you, is as foolish in polarity magic as it is in any other kind of relationship. Insisting that attraction ought to be present when it is not—whether that insistence is rooted in ideology, ego, or some other factor—is if anything more foolish, and will guarantee magical failure as well as other negative consequences.

Thus the presence or absence of mutual attraction, combined with a willingness on all sides to take the work seriously and abide by the necessary limits to physical affection, is the basic requirement for polarity magic. Ultimately, for you and your partner, it does not matter who Dion Fortune could or could not polarize with, or for that matter who some current ideology insists you ought to polarize with. What matters is simply whether you and your partner can polarize with each other. That, in turn, is best measured by gauging the emotional and erotic attraction that flows between you.

Twofold and fourfold patterns

The basic method of polarity working involves two participants. It is at least as common, however, to include other people in the work. On the one hand, it is considerably easier for two people to work polarity magic even at high levels of erotic and emotional energy, and not have those forces spill over into physical intimacy, when other people are present. On the other, having other trained participants involved in the working helps stabilize and strengthen the energy flows. While the primary partners provide the energy, additional participants help direct it toward its goal and keep it focused.

If you are interested in bringing in other people, four participants is a good minimum—in polarity working, as in relationships, the triangle is the least stable of patterns! For example, it is quite common for two couples, both happy in their current relationships, to practice polarity magic together. All four take part, but the attraction between a member of one couple and a member of the other is the primary motive force for the working. Since all four people are present and exchanging energy, this arrangement keeps jealousies to a minimum. That only works, of course, if both members of both couples are competent mages—which of course is not always the case.

Magical lodges and less formal group workings use this approach very often when polarity work is to be done. Even when there are more than four members of the lodge, one pair forms the primary line of energy, while a second pair at right angles to them stabilizes and directs the energy flow. Full instructions for workings of this kind are provided later in this book.

It works best if both of the pairs of partners in this form of work are linked by some level of emotional and erotic attraction, but this is less necessary for the secondary partners than for the primary couple.

For the secondary partners, almost any emotional response is enough to yield good results. Ordinary friendship can be quite adequate—and so can more difficult emotions.

One lodge I worked with, for example, had two members, both women, who happened to dislike each other intensely. They were both competent mages and decent human beings, and so they kept their feelings toward each other from interfering with lodge activities. The presiding officer of the lodge noted this, and put the two of them face to face as the secondary partners in lodge working, while he and the second officer of the lodge filled their usual role as primary partners. I have rarely witnessed a more powerful lodge working; the sheer emotional force generated by the two women, holding their mutual detestation in check, provided a spectacular boost to the ritual. This kind of working requires very skilled participants, and it tends to be unstable: one of the two women, in fact, left the lodge not long thereafter.

Dealing with excess sexual energy

Most of us have had the experience of dealing with unwanted erotic energy. Polarity workings, done effectively, are among the best ways to do that, but in the early stages of practice the complete sublimation of the erotic force does not always happen. Everyday life in today's societies very often leaves people in a state of sexual arousal with no convenient outlet. Masturbation is not always helpful—as noted in an earlier chapter, it tends to have unwanted effects on the etheric body. For both these reasons, it is useful to have a method to sublimate erotic energies without the help of a partner.

The occult literature has several such methods to offer. One that has proven useful for people of both sexes, as well as intersex persons, comes from one branch of the Rosicrucian tradition.[22] It is done as follows.

When you are feeling sexually aroused and choose not to express the arousal in the usual way, stand straight, tense your entire body lightly—not enough to cause strain, but enough that you feel the muscles engage from your feet up to your head. Place your hands with the palms an inch or two in front of your genitals, and concentrate on the thought that the sex power is about to rise to higher regions of your body, and be transmuted into spiritual force. Feel the sexual energy in your palms.

---

[22] Plummer 1923, p. 44.

Now slowly draw your hands slowly upwards on each side of the abdomen, following the natural curve of the body but staying an inch or so away from the skin. As you do so, feel the sexual energy rising with your hands, leaving the genital region completely. Bring the energy up to your nipples and feel it concentrate in the breast area. If your concentration is strong you will feel your breasts swell slightly and sense energy gathering in them; yes, this works equally well no matter what your biological sex may happen to be. This is the first stage, and the first few times you do this exercise, stop here.

Once you can reliably draw sexual energy up to the energy centers in your breasts, go on to the next stage. The next time you need to sublimate sexual energy, bring it up from the genitals over the breasts and keep going, until your hands are on either side of your throat. (Rotate the hands as needed so that your palms face your throat.) Feel the energy concentrating in the throat center. Here also you will feel the throat charged with pressure and energy. This is the second stage, and should be practiced until bringing sexual energy from genitals to throat is easy.

Once you can do this, proceed to the final stage. The next time after this that you need to sublimate sexual energy, bring the hands up from the genitals past the breasts and the throat, and then move your hands further so that your left hand is behind your head with the palm facing the back of the skull, and your right hand is in front of your head with the palm facing the spot between your two eyebrows. Feel the sexual energy charging the brain with vital force.

Once you have done this a few times, consult a book or website on the anatomy of the brain, locate the pineal gland and the pituitary gland, and thereafter imagine your left hand charging your pineal gland and your right hand charging your pituitary gland. These glands are of central importance in advanced magical practices, and gently stimulating them with unused sexual energy will help prepare you for these advanced workings.

Remember that the goal of this practice is to withdraw sexual arousal completely from the genital area and relocate the energy to higher centers in the body, where it can help you with your spiritual development. If any arousal remains in your genital area, repeat the exercise, and then turn your attention to something else. It helps if you avoid pornography, romance fiction, and other sources of sexual stimulation during times when you either do not have an outlet for your sexual desires or do not choose to make use of it. The point of this exercise is not to flirt with yourself in the "will I, won't I" manner, but to clear away sexual energy so that you can do something else with the energy and with your time.

The method just given requires some degree of mastery of the basic occult skills of concentration and visualization, and it also requires regular practice. It can be used for the practical goal of managing erotic desire, of course, but it also functions quite well as basic training for the work of polarity magic. If you can do this exercise effectively, sublimating your erotic energies so that you are no longer troubled by them, you have enough mastery of concentration, visualization, and direction of energy to get good results from a polarity working. If you have not yet reached that point, it may be worth considering putting more time into the basics of magical practice before you attempt advanced work of this kind.

Preparations for working

Some kinds of ceremonial magic are exceptionally complex. They require intricate astrological calculations, working tools and other material objects made to precise specifications, and lengthy ritual texts that must be committed to memory. Among the advantages of polarity magic is that it is relatively simple in terms of its requirements. In polarity magic, the working tools that matter are the wills and imaginations of the participants, and the erotic energies that flow naturally through their etheric and astral bodies.

All other equipment is secondary, and may be dispensed with if it interferes with the working. Those mages who enjoy making and using elaborate working tools, banners, robes, and the like can certainly get busy creating them, and those who work in traditions that require such things may put them to work as they wish, but the material requirements of polarity work are very simple. The workings given in the next two chapters have the following requirements.

- *The work takes place in a private working space large enough to accommodate the participants.* A working group consisting of two people can function very well in an ordinary room of modest size; a group with more members will of course need more space. The only requirements for the space, however, are a reasonable amount of quiet and a door that can be locked to provide privacy.

- *A chair will be needed for each participant.* The polarity workings given in this chapter are done entirely in a seated position, without any movement around the space. The chairs should therefore be comfortable enough that the participants can sit in them for the entire length of the polarity working without being distracted by physical discomforts.
- *Plain robes of any suitable color may be worn.* These are useful simply because they prevent distraction, and make it a little easier for the participants to set aside their personalities and function as vessels for impersonal cosmic forces. Ordinary street clothes make this state of impersonality harder to achieve, and ritual nudity is distracting and can make it more difficult to sublimate erotic energies and direct them toward the intention of the working.
- *All the participants need to have a good general knowledge of the same system of ceremonial magic, and engage in daily magical practice in that system.* If everyone involved in the workings is doing daily work with the same internal energy exercise, as discussed in the previous chapter, it will be much easier to get beyond the most basic levels of polarity work.
- *Finally, a single intention should be chosen, discussed, and kept in mind by all participants.* Magic, as noted earlier, is the art and science of causing changes in consciousness in accordance with will. That implies that every magical act is an act of will, and every act of will moves toward an intention. In the early stages of work, the intention can be as simple as mastering the art of polarity magic. Later on, as discussed below, other intentions can be pursued. In every working, however, the intention should be clear, and every person taking part in the working should know what it is and freely choose to direct will and imagination toward it.

Note also that the workings given below should be practiced within a space that has been purified and consecrated by some form of ceremonial magic. Any standard opening and closing ritual can be used for this purpose. If you practice magic in the tradition of the Hermetic Order of the Golden Dawn, for example, the standard solitary temple opening, including the Lesser Banishing Ritual of the Pentagram, purification with water, consecration with fire, triple circumambulation, and invocation of the Lord of the Universe, is very well suited to this form of work, and the corresponding closing ceremony can be used afterwards.

Other branches of the Golden Dawn tree, such as the Druidical Order of the Golden Dawn and the Fellowship of the Hermetic Rose, will find their own temple opening and closing rituals equally well suited to work of this kind. I have also done polarity workings in space prepared by the solitary grove rituals of two Druid orders, the Order of Bards Ovates and Druids (OBOD) and the Ancient Order of Druids in America (AODA), and the lodge ritual of the Golden Section Fellowship (GSF), with good results. My guess, though I have not had the chance to test this out with other opening and closing ceremonies, is that any other standard means of establishing magical space for ceremonial work will be equally effective as a frame for your polarity workings.[23]

Another point is worth making at this stage. The flow of energy in polarity workings can be strengthened and stabilized by aligning it with the currents of energy in the macrocosm. Here the standard approach is to have the couple working polarity magic sitting so that the partner with a male astral body is sitting in the east, and the partner with a female astral body is sitting in the west. Due to the rotation of the earth, there is a constant astral current moving from east to west, and aligning the working with that current helps amplify the effect. Since many systems of ceremonial magic align their lodges on an east–west axis, this is easy to work into most systems. If it is impossible to arrange, it can be done without; it is a help, not a strict requirement.

The workings in this book, like most of the practices of ceremonial magic, start with a basic ritual which functions as a template for the more complex and potent workings further on. The basic method given in the following chapter has two varieties, one for two persons, one for four. The two-person method is intended for workings when the two participants are the only ones present. The four-person method can be used for any group of four or more, though only four will take active roles: the two who are responsible for the core of the work, who are called the primary couple in this book, and two others, the secondary couple, whose task is to stabilize the working, so that the primary couple can direct all their efforts toward the intention of the working. Methods that involve active participation by many people are given in Chapter 8.

---

[23] If you do not know how to perform an opening and closing ceremony of this kind, learn one and practice it regularly for a year or so before you attempt polarity magic. Again, polarity work is not for beginners.

CHAPTER 6

Basic polarity magic

In approaching the practice of polarity magic, it is worth reiterating that the magic works by sublimating erotic energies, not by whipping them up into a frenzy. That point has been misplaced embarrassingly often in recent discussions of the subject. One book on polarity magic widely available a few years ago includes a ritual for two participants, a man and a woman, in which both are naked except for jewelry. They spend much of the ritual breathing on and kissing each other's erogenous zones—when, that is, one of them is not wriggling from head to foot over the top of the other's reclining body! This is foreplay, not polarity magic.[24]

Polarity magic of the kind this book teaches is considerably less blatant in its erotic dimension. The participants keep their clothing on, and do not come into physical contact at any point during the ceremony. The same currents of erotic energy that can make two people fall in love at first sight when they stand at opposite ends of a room is sublimated in polarity working and used to empower a chosen magical intention.

---

[24] I'm not suggesting that there is anything wrong with foreplay between consenting adults, of course. The point is simply that it belongs in the bedroom, not in the practice of polarity magic.

Seen from outside, the result can seem almost prim: two people in robes seated facing each other, neither one moving or speaking for long periods. Seen from within, it is an intense and highly intimate experience of participation in surging currents of power and life.

One further note is probably worth making here. While I have spent years studying the writings of Dion Fortune and her pupils on polarity magic, among other subjects, I am not a member of the Society of the Inner Light (SIL), the magical order she founded, and I do not have access to the specific rituals of polarity work taught privately to initiates of that organization. The workings described here, while informed by Fortune's work in many ways, take their basic form from a set of practices I received from the late John Gilbert, one of my occult teachers. How they compare to the SIL's practices will have to be judged by its initiates. What I can say is that these practices work well for a very wide range of magical purposes.

Basic two-person method

The basic method for two persons is as follows.

First, after the opening ceremony is finished, the participants sit at opposite ends of the working space, facing each other. The exact distance between the two participants can be worked out through experiment, but most people find that it should be more than three feet, so there is no sense of either person encroaching on the other's personal space, and less than twenty feet, so that the energy connection between the two participants is not too difficult to maintain. Both participants should take several minutes to relax all unnecessary tensions, and then use some form of simple rhythmic breathing to calm and stabilize the subtle bodies. The Fourfold Breath used in the Golden Dawn tradition—breathe in smoothly to the count of four, hold the breath in to the count of four, breath out smoothly to the count of four, and hold the breath out to the count of four—works well here, but so do other methods of breathwork.

Second, both participants awaken their palm centers in the way described in the previous chapter (pages 69–73).

Third, when both participants have awakened their palm centers, they raise their hands to shoulder level, palms facing the other participant, and concentrate on making contact. This is something that has to be learned through practice. The feeling of contact is distinctive: like bringing palms into physical contact, but subtler. When this has been achieved, many mages find that the connection can be strengthened by recalling what it feels like to take the hand of someone they love, and imagining that same feeling in their palms. With practice, imagination gives way to reality, and the same flow of polarity that links lovers through their hands links partners in polarity work.

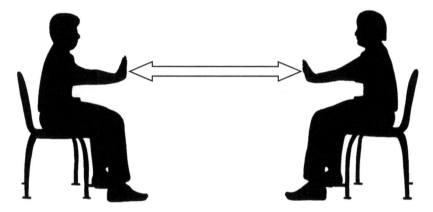

In the first stage, the flow of erotic energy is from palm to palm.

Contact between palm centers

Fourth, while maintaining the sense of contact between palms, both participants rotate their hands and arms out to the side and down to approximately hip level. When this movement is complete the arms are extended at an angle out and down from the shoulders. The palms of each participant face those of the other, and the flow of energy continues between them.

Fifth, each participant extends a beam or current of energy from their own solar plexus to the solar plexus of the other, and establishes the same feeling of contact between solar plexus and solar plexus that was achieved earlier between palm and palm. This is a more intimate connection and should be given time to establish itself. Once contact has been established, many mages find that the connection can be strengthened by recalling what it feels like to touch the bare body of someone they love, and imagining that feeling in their solar plexus. Once again, with practice, imagination gives way to reality, and the main current of polarity begins to flow.

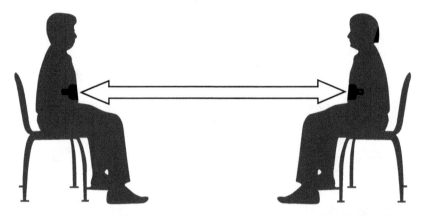

In the second stage, while the flow between the palms continues, the main flow of erotic energy is between solar plexus and solar plexus.

Contact between solar plexus centers

Sixth, once both participants feel the contact and the flow of polarity between them, they both imagine a second beam or current of energy streaming up from the solar plexus at an angle to a point above and midway between them. Where the two currents meet above, they form an image of the sun, which radiates light, warmth, and blessing down on both participants and on the entire working space. Once this is established, both participants concentrate on maintaining the entire pattern of visualization: the beams or currents connecting palm to palm as well as those connecting solar plexus to solar plexus, and both solar plexes to the sun shining above, as shown in the accompanying diagram. This may be maintained for as long as both participants choose.

Seventh, when it is time to close the working, the participants dissolve the image of the sun overhead and the two beams or currents of force rising to it. They then focus for a short time on the contact from solar plexus to solar plexus established in the fifth step. At this time it is important to let all remaining erotic and romantic energy flow into the current and be discharged into the other participant, so that no sexual or emotional tension remains.

Eighth, the participants then dissolve the connection from solar plexus to solar plexus, and rotate the hands back up to shoulder level, retaining the contact between them. They then focus for a short time on the connection established in the third step.

In the third stage, the polarity unfolds into a ternary and awakens higher modalities of energy on the etheric, astral, and higher planes.

The completed circuit

Ninth, the participants break the connection between the palms, and close the palm centers using the method in step 8 (c) in the previous chapter (pages 73–74). This completes the working, and is followed by the closing ceremony.

Commentary

This simple but effective working makes a good introduction to polarity magic, and should be learned first and practiced regularly by anyone who wants to explore the practical dimensions of this book. The work begins with you and your partner making contact through the palm centers. This is a less intimate connection than the solar plexus contact that follows—it is like holding hands, as compared to more intimate forms of physical contact—and many people find that time spent in this stage allows them to relax into the working and allow the energy to flow more easily in the rest of the working. Notice that each participant's right hand faces the left hand of the other. This establishes between you and your partner the same palm-to-palm polarity that is used to awaken the palm centers.

Once the currents between the palms are well established, the palms rotate out and down, away from the midline of the body, to allow free play to the solar plexus contact. It is at this point that the real work of polarity magic begins. The erotic and emotional attraction you feel for your partner in the working is to flow into your solar plexus and through the channel uniting them. Some people find it very easy to do this, others must practice it repeatedly to get the desired effect. It has much the same feeling as entering into an embrace, and has the same degree of intimacy, even though no physical contact takes place.

If you have trouble learning how to do it, the most important rule to keep in mind is not to try to force it. Open yourself to the twofold flow, outward from your solar plexus to your partner's and inward from your partner's to yours; let it happen, don't make it happen. It may seem very faint at first, and it may seem to be going all one way, depending on your sensitivity to the astral and etheric planes. Don't worry if either of these happens. With time and practice, you will be able to feel the two-way flow clearly. Later, as you and your partner become used to the flow of energy, the astrally active partner can push the energy and the astrally receptive partner can pull it. This can amplify the flow to a dramatic degree.

Let the currents of energy flowing between you and your partner flow unhindered for a time before you move on to the sixth step, the formulation of the triadic structure and the awakening of the Inner Sun. Like lovemaking, the process of polarity working should not be rushed! The stronger and more stable the flow between the participants becomes, the more power will come into manifestation once the Inner Sun is envisioned.

Finally, for the same reason, take your time in the closing phases. The goal is to finish the working in a calm and relaxed state, with all excess erotic energy released and the subtle bodies of both participants balanced and gently energized.

Basic four-person method

The basic method for four persons is as follows.

First, once the opening ceremony is completed, the primary couple sit at opposite ends of the working space, facing each other. The secondary couple sit facing each other at right angles to the primary couple. (Thus, for example, if the primary couple are sitting in the east and west of the working space, the secondary couple are sitting in the north and south.) The participants should take several minutes to relax all unnecessary tensions, and then use some form of simple rhythmic breathing to calm and stabilize the subtle bodies, as described above.

Second, the primary couple awaken their palm centers in the way described in the previous chapter (pages 69–73).

Third, when both members of the primary couple have awakened their palm centers, they raise their hands to shoulder level, palms facing each other, and concentrate on making contact as explained in the description of the two-person method above. While they do this, the secondary couple awaken their palm centers in the way given earlier.

Fourth, both members of the secondary couple raise their hands to shoulder level, angled outwards, so that each of them has one hand facing one member of the primary couple and one hand facing the other member of the primary couple. The members of the primary couple then rotate their own palms outwards, releasing the palm-to-palm contact with each other and establishing it with the two members of the secondary couple. The result is a square or diamond of polarity flow, as shown in the diagram of the diamond of forces. This can be tricky, since the forces are not passing directly from partner to partner but indirectly, through the mediation of the other pair of partners. Especially in the early stages of training, it is usually best to take ample time to let this become stable and firm.

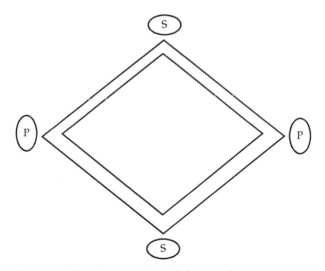

P represents the primary partners, S the secondary.

Diamond of forces

Fifth, the members of the primary couple now extend a beam or current of energy directly from solar plexus to solar plexus, and establish the feeling of contact between solar plexus and solar plexus. (The secondary couple do not establish such a connection, since their role is to stabilize the forces worked by the primary couple.) The pattern of polarity flow now becomes a square with a line on the diagonal, the symbol of generation in sacred geometry, as shown in the diagram below. This pattern should be given ample time to become strong and stable before moving to the next step, and all the points discussed in the two-person method relating to the flow between the two solar plexus centers should be kept in mind here as well.

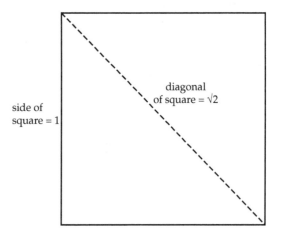

Square and diagonal

Sixth, once the pattern of flow is stable and strong, both members of the primary couple imagine a second beam or current of energy streaming up from the solar plexus at an angle to a point above and midway between them. Where the two currents meet above, as in the two-person working, they form an image of the sun, which radiates light and warmth down on both participants and on the entire working space. The members of the secondary couple also visualize and feel the same pattern, which forms the equilateral triangle, the symbol of harmonious form in sacred geometry, rising up out of the square of stability and the diagonal line of generation. Once this is established, the whole pattern of forces should be visualized as clearly and intensely as possible. This may be maintained for as long as the participants choose.

Seventh, when it is time to close the working, the participants dissolve the image of the sun overhead and the two beams or currents of force rising to it. The primary couple focuses for a short time on the contact from solar plexus to solar plexus established in the fifth step, releasing all erotic and romantic energy in the process, while the secondary couple focuses on maintaining the square established in the fourth step.

Eighth, the primary couple then dissolves the connection from solar plexus to solar plexus, and rotate the hands inward, dissolving the square and restoring the contact between them. They then focus for a short time on the connection established in the third step. Meanwhile the secondary couple also dissolves the square and closes their palm centers, using the method described in the previous chapter.

Ninth, the members of the primary couple then break the connection between their palms, and close the palm centers using the method in step 8 (c) in the previous chapter (pages 73–74). This completes the working, and is followed by the closing ceremony.

Commentary

This pattern is very nearly identical to the two-person method. The primary difference is that the two additional participants provide a stabilizing factor, so that considerably more energy can be handled. All the comments made in the discussion of the two-person working should be kept in mind here as well.

Students of sacred geometry will likely have noticed already that the four-person method is set up to use a particular set of geometrical symbolism, as shown in the diagram above. One of the basic principles in sacred geometry is the square root of 2 ($\sqrt{2}$), the ratio between the side and diagonal of a square. Another is the square root of 3 ($\sqrt{3}$), the ratio between the height and width of a vesica, which is formed by two equal circles with their centers on each other's circumference, and is the geometrical figure used to construct an equilateral triangle. The square is established in step 4 of the four-person method, and the diagonal is established between the primary couple in step 5. The triangle is established in step 6. In sacred geometry, the $\sqrt{2}$ ratio is a symbol of generation while the $\sqrt{3}$ ratio is a symbol of integration, and of course this is exactly what happens to the erotic energy in the working: it is generated by the participants, and then integrated into a structure of balanced energy and intention.

During the working, these two principles are assigned to the two couples. The secondary couple works with the √2 principle; they pay attention to each other, even though they do not visualize a current of energy linking them directly. The polarity between them follows an indirect path, moving by the square through the primary couple, and this generates much of the energy that flows through the working. The primary couple works with the √3 principle; their task is to integrate the energy directly, using a threefold structure that unites them with the visualized sun overhead.

More than four persons

The same methods can be used with a larger number of people, but the same division into primary and secondary partnerships is retained, and the other participants become a third category of supporting mages. This is standard practice in many magical lodges that work with polarity. In one common scheme, as shown in the lodge polarity diagram, the primary polarity flows between the chief mage of the lodge and his or her assistant at the other end of the lodge room, the secondary flows are maintained by assistant mages at the midpoints of the long sides, and the other members who are present assist by concentrating on building and maintaining the imagery of the working and filling other ceremonial roles.

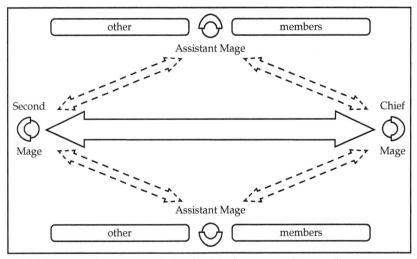

The solid arrow is the primary polarity, the dotted arrows are the secondary energy flows from palm to palm.

Lodge polarity

One advantage of this approach is that it provides the opportunity for inexperienced practitioners to come into contact with polarity work and gain some sense of how it functions before having to take a primary or secondary role in the working. The downside of this advantage is that beginners can be overwhelmed by even so indirect an exposure to the energies awakened by polarity workings. It has happened that novice members who professed a great enthusiasm for magical work quit a lodge after one experience of polarity work along these lines, or even bolted for the door halfway through the working. Not everyone who claims to be interested in magic is prepared to deal with its reality!

For this reason polarity workings of this kind are usually best restricted to the higher degrees worked by a magical lodge. This will allow beginners to get comfortable with the energies awakened in less intensive forms of magical work, and to practice the basic disciplines of the tradition themselves for some time, before being exposed to forces that may be more than they are emotionally prepared to handle.

Similar issues come up routinely whenever new people are brought into an existing working group, whether or not the group uses the formal organization of a magical lodge and whether or not polarity magic is worked in the group. Most occultists with any experience of group working have watched an apparently promising student bolt for the door, literally or figuratively, when magic turns out to be more real than they expected. Polarity working, because of its power and its intimacy, tends to get this reaction a little more often than other forms of magic, and practitioners should be aware that this is always a risk.

Three practical applications

The first task of any novice practitioner of polarity magic is to learn one or both of the basic methods given earlier in this chapter. Only when at least one of these has been practiced regularly until it can be done from memory, without any of the participants having to fumble with a book to remember the next step, should anything more be attempted.

Once a basic method has been mastered, however, certain kinds of practical magic come within reach. Three of them are given here: a ritual of earth blessing, which can be used to bring healing energies to bear on the land in a given area; a ritual of consecration, which can be used to charge and empower a talisman or a magical working tool; and a ritual of scrying, which uses polarity to amplify the human capacity for clairvoyance and help bring about clearer, more detailed, and more intense visionary experiences. All of these work with slight variations of the basic methods covered above. All of them require some knowledge of ceremonial magic more generally, but of course this is true of all forms of polarity magic.

A ritual of earth blessing

This working can be used either as a way of directing healing energy toward the earth as a whole, or in a more focused way to bless and heal the land in a specific area, either to remove negative influences that have become entrenched in the area or to prepare the location of a temple or some other sacred place. It is especially effective for clearing away the lifeless, devitalized quality so often brought about by the abuse of the land in modern industrial societies.

Begin by settling on a specific intention for the working. All participants should spend some time meditating on the intention before the working is performed. The participants should also choose a symbol to represent the energies that will be directed into the earth. This can be any general symbol of blessing and life, or it may be something more specific. Divination can be used if necessary to select an appropriate symbol.

Issues of magical timing may also be worth considering. There are many ways of timing a magical working, ranging across the scale of complexity from observation of the moon's phases through the planetary hours to full-blown electional astrology, in which a horoscope is cast to choose a time for a ritual working in which all the celestial factors will be aligned with its intention. All these can be applied effectively to polarity magic; using some method of timing the working is not essential, but it can pay off considerably in making the work more effective.

To perform this working, begin with an opening ceremony and then whatever ritual methods you prefer to use to formulate the intention of a magical working. For example, if you and your partner are using Golden Dawn magic, you might open the temple in the usual way, proclaim the intention of the working, invoke an appropriate elemental or planetary force using the Ritual of the Pentagram or Hexagram corresponding to that force, and then trace the same pentagram or hexagram above the altar, vibrate the appropriate divine name, and draw in and circulate the force using the vibratory formula of the Middle Pillar.[25]

---

[25] All these techniques are given in detail in Regardie 2015 and Greer 2017.

Other systems of ceremonial magic have their own methods for formulating and intention and charging it with power, and these can be used instead if you work with a different system.

Once this is finished, proceed with either of the two basic methods through the end of step six. Once the sun overhead is visualized and empowered with a current of energy, the next phase of the work begins. This involves charging the image of the sun with as much erotic energy as the participants can put into it. In the four-person working, the primary couple carry out the charging, while the secondary couple maintain the square of balanced forces and pour as much of their own erotic tension as they can into the process. All four participants visualize the image of the sun, however, and imagine the symbol chosen for the operation standing in the sun. With practice, the sun will feel to all present as though it is the focus of steadily building pressure, like the pressure of erotic energy rising toward orgasm. Do not rush this stage; the longer it can be continued without losing focus, the stronger the working will be.

When the pressure reaches its zenith, one participant gives a signal—a simple nod of the head is suitable—and the energy that has built up in the image of the sun is allowed to discharge straight down into the earth in a single intense ray of force. The symbol chosen for the working is visualized as descending with the discharge and entering into the earth. This stage again should not be rushed. Most of the energy will descend in the initial discharge, but not all, and the remainder should be allowed to follow the path of discharge into the earth. This will make the working more effective, and also more satisfying for the participants.

Once the energies have been fully released into the earth, proceed from step seven to the end of the working. Proclaim the working successfully completed, and then close using whatever closing ritual you have chosen.

A ritual of consecration

The art of consecrating talismans and magical working tools is an important part of most systems of ceremonial magic, and the formula just outlined is an effective way of doing this. Here the polarity working is best added to the standard methods of consecration, whatever those happen to be in the tradition in which you are working. In addition to the talisman or working tool, a piece of silk or linen suitable for wrapping it, and the other requirements of the ritual, you will need to choose a symbol for the energy you will be directing into the consecration. For example, if you are consecrating a talisman of Jupiter, the planetary emblem of Jupiter is appropriate, while if you are consecrating a pentacle of earth, the symbol of the element of earth may be used. Any symbol or sigil appropriate to the work and to the system of magic you practice may be used here.

As before, perform the opening ceremony, proclaim the intention of the working, use whatever methods of invoking magical and spiritual force your tradition of ceremonial magic provides, purify and consecrate the talisman or working tool in some way, and then set it in the center of the working space, preferably on an altar covered with an altar cloth.

Once this is done, proceed just as in the ritual of earth blessing just given up to the end of step six. Charge the image of the sun with erotic energy in the same way, placing the symbol in the sun, and building up the energy in the image of the sun to the greatest intensity the participants can handle in a controlled fashion. When you allow the energy to discharge, however, direct all of it into the talisman or working tool. If the ritual is at all effective, all the participants may need to concentrate on leading the energy where it should go and keeping it there; the energy flows can be very unruly.

Once the talisman or working tool is charged, one of the participants should go to the central altar and wrap the consecrated item in silk or linen, so that the energies placed in it will not be discharged by the closing ritual and any banishing rituals that may be part of that. If circumstances permit, the item can also be placed in a box or other container and removed from the altar for this same purpose. The rest of the working is done exactly as given in the two- or four-person methods, and is followed by the closing ritual.

This ritual can be repeated many times with the same item, with excellent results. Repeated consecrations of the same talisman or working tool increase its power considerably—and of course repeated practice of the same ritual is always helpful as a way of developing skill in any form of practical magic.

A ritual of scrying

This ritual works with a pattern of energy flow somewhat different from the one used in the basic two- and four-person workings. The most significant energy center in the human body for clairvoyant function is the third eye or pituitary center, which is located just above the bridge of the nose and between the eyebrows. The scrying ritual works with this center as well as the solar plexus and palm centers.

This is most often done as a two-person working, even when other participants are available, because many people find the privacy and intimacy of a two-person working more comfortable for the practice of psychism. For most people, this ritual allows a far more intense and powerful experience than ordinary scrying, and that increased intensity should be taken into account when preparing for the work and its aftermath.

To perform this ritual, however, both partners should have ample experience with scrying or, as it is also called, active imagination. A few pathworkings done in a group setting, following along half-passively while someone else reads a written description, is not enough! A year or so of weekly practice for both partners with the Golden Dawn method of scrying in the spirit vision, Jungian active imagination, or some similar method is adequate. It is important that this training focus on visionary work without a prepared script, so that both of you will be ready to deal with unexpected experiences on the inner planes.

You and your partner will need to agree on a theme or target for the working. Published accounts of workings of this kind among Dion Fortune's students suggest that it was standard practice in those circles to use methods of this kind to recover memories of past lives or to recover the details of magical workings in the distant past.[26] This is only one of the many possible applications of this ritual, however. It can equally well be used to make contact with elemental, planetary, and Sephirothic planes, for example, or to interact with spiritual beings on their own planes rather than summoning them to appear on ours.

You and your partner will also want to decide in advance which of you will take the lead in the visionary journey. When both members of a working polarity partnership are experienced in this form of scrying, this can be dispensed with, but in the beginning it works best for one person to lead the experience and narrate the visionary journey that results, while the other person makes an effort where necessary to see the same things and attune to the same experiences as the leader. It often works best for the leader's role to alternate between the partners from one session to the next.

---

[26] See Richardson 1985, and Richardson and Hughes 1992.

After the opening ceremony, the ritual follows the first five steps in the basic two-person method exactly. In place of step six, though, the ritual proceeds as follows:

Sixth, you and your partner maintain the flow of energy between the solar plexus centers, and establish another connection between your third eye centers. To do this, both partners imagine a third eye opening just above the bridge of the nose, above and between the two material eyes. The two newly opened eyes gaze into each other, and a current of energy develops between them. This current will feel considerably subtler than the one between the solar plexus centers, and will flow in the opposite direction: for example, if the flow at solar plexus level runs from the astrally active partner to the astrally receptive one, the flow at third eye level will run from the receptive to the active partner.

Seventh, once the connection at the third eye level is established, link the currents at third eye and solar plexus level. This is done by imagining a channel inside the body connecting the solar plexus center with the middle of the head, and then bending forward to the third eye center. Once both partners have done this, the erotic forces will begin to flow in circuit, passing from one partner to the other, going up or down through the channel, and then flowing back the other way. Let the flow of energies in this circuit of force establish itself and become steady and strong, so that both partners' third eye centers will be well activated.

Eighth, go into the vision. Depending on the theme of your work, this may involve any of several different techniques. The visualization of falling together down a well, which Colonel Seymour and Christine Campbell Thompson used to reach back in time and see visions of the distant past, is very useful for getting visions of past lives or ancient times. To come into contact with beings of superhuman spiritual capacities, the opposite approach—rising up through a well of light into ever brighter illumination—can be more effective. Some people also find it works well simply to make a mental effort to be in the scene desired. As with any form of clairvoyance, this may or may not produce the kind of vivid imagery that appears to be objectively real. If this doesn't happen, don't worry: if the images you get are like the images you experience in memory and daydreaming, that can be just as effective for magical purposes.

Ninth, as soon as the visionary work begins, the person who is leading begins to describe in a clear voice exactly what he or she is perceiving. The other partner tries to see the same things as clearly as possible. Very often, once both partners have developed some skill in the practice, they will find themselves seeing the same thing before a word is said! Proceed with the scrying in the usual manner from this point on.

Tenth, when the visionary experience is finished, both partners return in consciousness to their material bodies in the chairs. Once this is complete, dissolve the current of force connecting the two third eye centers, releasing the circuit of force, and redirect attention to the solar plexus centers and the current connecting them. Pause for a little while, and then proceed with the seventh, eighth, and ninth steps of the basic two-person method before closing with the closing ceremony.

Other practical workings

The three rituals just given are far from the only types of workings that can be done with the basic formulas already given. It can be a very useful training exercise to go through the standard ritual workings presented by whatever system of ceremonial magic you know how to use, identifying ways in which the basic methods can be put to work in them. Plan on doing at least three or four practical workings using the basic methods, either following the rituals just given or creating your own from the material of the system of ceremonial magic in which you are trained, before going on to the more advanced workings of the following chapters.

CHAPTER 7

Advanced polarity magic

The practical methods given in the previous chapter are quite adequate for most ordinary magical workings and can be developed in a great many ways. Two directions for further development are worth discussing here. The first is working with gods and heroes in polarity magic; the second is combining vertical and horizontal polarity in the same working. Both of these can be tricky. As noted already, therefore, it is best to get some familiarity with the more basic forms of practice before adding in one or both of these methods.

Work with gods and heroes and work with vertical and horizontal polarity have a common theme. The methods presented in the previous chapter work with polarity at the microcosmic level, directing the energies awakened by the sublimated erotic and emotional attraction between two people into magical work. These further dimensions of practice both draw in polarized forces from the macrocosm to empower the play of forces in the microcosm. If this is done with any degree of competence, it results in a much more robust working—but the mental, emotional, and physical consequences tend to be equally robust.

For this reason, *do not take up these workings until and unless you, your partner, and any other participants in the work are sure you can cope with the consequences.* A considerable amount of psychological and emotional maturity, a reasonable degree of physical health, and a solid knowledge of operative occultism, including methods to clear your material and subtle bodies of unwanted energies and influences, are essential in order to do this work with any degree of safety. It is also essential that you have done a reasonable amount of practice with the basic polarity workings already presented in this book, so that you and your partner are used to sublimating erotic and romantic attraction and directing the energy they unlock toward magical intentions. These basic techniques of practice should be routine for everyone concerned before you proceed to the advanced methods.

Gods and godforms

Magic and religion are not the same thing, but both involve interactions with deities. Some of those interactions follow much the same pattern in magic as in religion. It is very common, for example, for mages to pray to the deities they worship in the course of a magical working, asking for blessings on their work and for the downrush of power from the higher planes of being that raises magic above the limits of the merely human. It is of course possible to include such prayers in the simpler kinds of polarity working already introduced in this book, and many systems of ceremonial magic do this as a matter of course.

The most important method of working with gods and goddesses used in polarity magic is a little different, and requires considerably more skill and practice to handle effectively. This is the method of assuming a godform, as it is called in some schools of magic. The point of the method is easy to misunderstand, and so a certain amount of explanation will be useful before we go on to the technical details.

Human beings are not deities. It is possible under some circumstances, however, for human beings to become the vehicles for the manifestation of divine energies. In sacramental Christian churches, for example, the priest functions as a vehicle for the presence and power of Christ, especially in the ceremony of communion. The Christian monastic exercise of the imitation of Christ has some of the same intention; the person who practices it sets out to embody as much of the living presence of Christ as he or she can.

In esoteric traditions of Buddhism such as the Shingon sect of Japan, similarly, monks and nuns are taught to visualize themselves in meditation as a buddha or bodhisattva—that is to say, one of the holy beings of the esoteric Buddhist tradition. The point of this practice is not to inflate the ego, but to embody the state of consciousness exemplified by the buddha or bodhisattva, in the same spirit that the devout Christian seeks to embody the spirit of Christ. It is a powerful practice and can lead to profoundly transformative experiences.

The magical practice of assuming a godform is similar in its spirit to these examples, and closely related in its technique to the last of them. The mage who chooses to practice it starts by choosing the traditional image of a deity and learning every detail of that image. The gods and goddesses of ancient Egypt are very commonly used for work of this kind, because their images were worked out precisely in very ancient times and copied exactly for thousands of years thereafter. Other deities can of course be worked with in this way, though it helps if the deity you revere has a detailed traditional image.

Once the image has been learned thoroughly, the mage enters into meditation and imagines himself or herself as the deity. This involves, first, imagining your body as the body of the deity, in as vivid and detailed a manner as possible; second, imagining your mind as the mind of the deity, thinking the thoughts and feeling the feelings appropriate to the deity; and third, calling down the spirit of the deity into you, so that you become a temporary vessel for the living presence of the deity. This is not mediumship; the mage practicing it does not go into trance, but instead retains full conscious awareness the whole time. In the process of this work, the mage's body, mind, and spirit are purified, empowered, and made more like that of the deity.

Before you can use this method effectively in magical workings, you need to perform it many times as an independent practice. It is important to learn how to take on a godform, and just as important to learn how to release it again: to let go of the awareness of the divine spirit, then to let go of the deity's thoughts and feelings so that you can return to your own, and finally to dissolve the imagined form of the god or goddess so that you experience your body as it is, not as a vehicle for a divine presence. Regular practice will make this easy.

Furthermore, you will need to put in some degree of personal practice with every deity whose godform you choose to take on. Being able to take on the godform of Osiris with good results does not guarantee that you can do the same thing just as well with the godform of Horus, say, or Thoth. Each deity is a unique divine person, and you will need to attune yourself with that divine person before you can become a vessel for his or her energies in ritual.

This is especially important in polarity magic using godforms, for a simple reason: you need to pay attention to polarity relationships between deities as well as between human participants. Deities are not abstractions, nor are they appliances for human beings to use however they like. They are divine persons, and they have their own relationships and desires, which can be found chronicled at great length in traditional mythologies. The ancient priesthoods crafted mythic narratives with exquisite care to express the nature of the gods and goddesses they served, and it is always wise to follow their guidance in workings such as these.

One further warning is appropriate here. Don't think that you can tinker with mythologies by changing the orientation of deities to suit your preferences, and get good results. For example, it is never a good idea to try to bring a nonsexual deity in a polarity working! When the creators of ancient mythologies defined Minerva, for example, as a virgin goddess, they were not simply telling a story. They were using the symbolism of human sexual relationships to say something specific and important about Minerva. One important implication they meant to pass on is that Minerva does not polarize with any other deity. (Nor, for that matter, was she generated by a polarity relationship between deities—this is one meaning of the myth that has her born from the head of Jupiter.) The blowback from trying to force a polarity working on a nonpolarizing deity may or may not be swift, but it will be highly unwelcome.

Similar issues arise in trying to force a deity whose myths focus on relationships with the other sex into same-sex relationships, or for that matter vice versa. Deities, like humans, have their own distinctive orientations. It makes perfect sense, in fact, to think of some deities as heterosexual, some as homosexual, some as bisexual, and some as asexual. There are male deities, female deities, intersex deities, and deities who are known to change their genders from time to time. It's at least as important to recognize the real diversities, sexes, and orientations of deities as it is to recognize the same things in human beings—especially but not only in the practice of polarity magic.

Thus the best approach to working with deities in polarity magic is to choose deities who have a sexual relationship in mythology. A classic example from Egyptian mythology is the pairing of Osiris and Isis, since their love for each other is a central theme in the old myths of Egypt. Each member of the polarity partnership, in a two-person working, or the primary partnership, in a four-person working, then concentrates on learning to take on the godform of one of these polarized deities. In a two-person working, once both participants can do this effectively, the ritual working can proceed. In a four-person working, the secondary partners should learn to take on other godforms appropriate to the work, which need not have any sexual polarity between them—for example, if the primary partners are working with the godforms of Isis and Osiris, the secondary partners can take on the godforms of Horus and Anubis if they choose, or those of any other deities relevant to the specific working. Once all four participants can take on their godforms effectively, the work can proceed.

Heroes and hero forms

It is also possible to take the same methods and use them with important figures of legend. In ancient Greece, human beings who had risen above the limits of ordinary humanity and become the focus for reverence and ritual were called heroes—that's where the English word comes from—and this term makes a good label for the legendary figures under discussion. The art of taking on hero forms, like that of taking on godforms, can be an effective source of power for polarity magic as well as other magical arts. The same three-stage process described in the previous section for taking on godforms can be used equally to take on hero forms.

Unlike deities, heroes are not primary sources of life and power in the cosmos. They receive much of the power they have from the emotional energy that has been directed toward them by living human beings down through the years. Every culture has legendary figures who have become potent images in the collective imagination of a people, and these images can be used in polarity magic with powerful results. It is wholly irrelevant whether or not the legendary person in question ever existed as a living person; what matters is that he or she functions as a focus for human emotions and collective meanings.

Consider Robin Hood, the great outlaw of English legend. Two hundred years of careful research by British folklorists have failed to turn up any conclusive evidence that there ever was such a person. Nonetheless, everyone who grew up in the English-speaking world knows instinctively who Robin Hood was and what he represents in the collective imagination. As a focus for magical workings appropriate to his character—for example, workings for liberty and justice—he is capable of generating and directing considerable magical forces.

Robin Hood also belongs to the subset of legendary figures whose legends include explicit polarity relationships. A polarity working using the hero form of Robin Hood would therefore pair him with Maid Marian. The partners in a two-person working would therefore practice taking on these hero forms; the primary partners in a four-person working would do the same, while the secondary partners might practice taking on the hero forms of Little John and Friar Tuck respectively. (As with godforms, the forms taken on by the secondary partners need not be sexually polarized.)

Since hero forms are generally less potent and less personalized than godforms, it is possible to be a little more flexible with forms that do not have a polarity relationship in myth. Consider Johnny Appleseed, one of the enduring figures of American legend. Unlike Robin Hood, he was a well-documented historical person—his real name was John Chapman, and his grave in Fort Wayne, Indiana is visited by thousands of tourists every year—but his legendary image as a joyous, mystically inspired wanderer planting apple trees across the old frontier makes him a powerful hero form for certain kinds of magical work in the United States. As far as anyone knows, he was a lifelong celibate, but polarity workings pairing him with a feminine Spirit of the Wilderness can generate a great deal of force for workings of appropriate types.

It can be to the advantage of less experienced polarity mages to do a series of workings with appropriate hero forms before taking on the higher intensity of godform work. This advantage is balanced, however, by certain disadvantages. First of all, legendary heroes and heroines are more narrowly focused in terms of their magical potential than gods and goddesses. Robin Hood and Maid Marian are very well suited to certain kinds of magic—workings for liberty, for example, or for justice, or for anything having to do with wilderness and nonhuman nature—but there are plenty of other intentions for which they would be effectively inert. Call on hero forms only for intentions that reflect the legends in which that hero features: this rule will be found well worth following in this kind of work.

These days, however, it's embarrassingly common to hear people on all sides of the political landscape brandishing words like "justice" or "liberty" when what they really mean is winning crass material advantages for their economic class or political party at the expense of someone else. This is risky enough to do when gods are involved, but doing it with a hero form associated with justice or liberty risks blowback on a monumental scale. A polarity working that invoked Robin Hood and Maid Marian in the name of justice, when the real goal was to give unfair economic or political advantages to some group in society, would likely generate a thumping magical backlash, for the spirits of Robin Hood and Maid Marian would mete out actual justice in a way the mages who did the working would find exquisitely unwelcome. The rule here is that if you invoke justice, liberty, or any other abstract concept, be very sure that you really do want what you're asking for, because either way you'll get it.

Finally, just as gods and goddesses have their own orientations and desires, legends have their own momentum. It's never wise to invoke figures out of a legend unless you're sure you will be comfortable ending up where the legend will take you—and no, it emphatically does not work to retcon a legend to give it the ending you want.[27]

One embarrassing example I witnessed some years ago was a marriage ceremony that the couple designed around the legend of True Thomas and the Fairy Queen. In the original legend, Thomas spent seven years with the queen, and then was sent away when the queen took a new lover. The couple decided to rewrite the legend so that the two reunited and lived happily ever after, and built the entire wedding around that theme. Predictably, the attempted revision didn't work. Seven years after the ceremony, right on schedule, the wife fell in love with someone else and the marriage promptly and permanently blew apart.

This sort of blowback is anything but rare these days. One specific set of stories is responsible for the lion's (or rather the Pendragon's) share of these: the Arthurian legends. It is too often forgotten that the story of King Arthur is ultimately a story of failure. It is the tale of

---

[27] Retcon: internet slang for retroactive continuity, the process of changing the details of an established character to make the character fit a new story. However useful retconning may be for writers, it makes for ineffective magic because the older version generally has much more power than the retconned one.

a bright dream irrevocably destroyed by the personal weaknesses of the people who were assigned the task of upholding it. This pattern is hardwired into the core legend. Trying to ignore it or rewrite it out of existence will not change that, nor will it lead to any other outcome.

Mind you, it's quite possible to do effective polarity magic using any of the peripheral legends that have gathered around the story of Arthur. I know of very effective workings of this kind done with the central polarities of the Grail legend and the legend of Merlin, for example. Magical work that involves the polarity between Arthur and Guinevere or Lancelot and Guinevere, on the other hand, results reliably in failure. Unless failure is your goal, this is one set of legendary figures worth avoiding in polarity magic.

It is probably also worth discussing the use of contemporary fiction and media in this form of working. To a certain extent, novels, movies, television shows, comic books and even video games fill some of the roles in modern society that myths and legends filled in earlier times. Some characters from these sources have become the focus for a great deal of human emotion and can end up carrying important collective meanings. They can therefore function as hero forms in polarity magic and other forms of esoteric work.

This is not simply a theoretical possibility. Magical workings using literary creations such as the tentacled Great Old Ones of H.P. Lovecraft's Cthulhu mythos, characters from comic books, and other fictional creations have been performed by occultists tolerably often during the last half century with considerable effect.[28] I once successfully evoked the hero form of Batman to visible appearance, for that matter, and found it quite as powerful as some of the legendary hero forms I've worked with.

Two cautions are worth bringing up here, however. The first is that it takes time to build up a significant charge of power in a literary creation. Legendary figures get much of their force from the fact that they have been fed by the daydreams and emotional reactions of people for many generations. Characters from current pop-culture media haven't had that advantage, and the pool of energy on which they can draw is

---

[28] The Lovecraftian workings of Michael Bertiaux on the one hand, and Kenneth Grant on the other, are well known in modern occult circles; see Bertiaux 1988, and Grant 1992 and 1994.

often very shallow. Those characters and images that have been popular for more than one generation tend to be considerably more potent.

The second caution is that characters from legends tend to be ideal types, while characters from modern pop culture are not. Unlike the old legends, our fiction, movies, and other media very often focus on characters who are emotionally troubled or psychologically unbalanced to a greater or lesser degree. Whatever the literary value of this, it makes such characters potentially problematic in magic, because participants who invoke these hero forms in magical work will tend to become more like the characters they invoke, for good or ill. You can give yourself emotional troubles or psychological imbalances very readily this way.

As a general rule, I recommend avoiding pop-culture characters in polarity magic unless you are thoroughly experienced in working with gods and legendary heroes, and your emotional and psychological balance is good. Even then, workings of this kind should be considered experimental until much more work has been done with them.

Working with god or hero forms

We will assume at this point that you have navigated your way through the various dangers pointed out already in this chapter, selected a pair of godforms or hero forms that polarize well together in myth or legend, and practiced working with them until you can reliably sense the power and consciousness of the god or goddess, or the energy of the hero or heroine, that you have decided to invoke. What then?

The methods discussed in the previous chapter are the templates to use for polarity workings in this chapter as well. The difference is simply that you take on the godforms or hero forms, and those forms—rather than your material bodies—become the vehicles for the flow of polarity magic. In either the two-person or four-person form of working, the assumption of the godforms or hero forms takes place between steps one and two of the ceremonies as given. At this point, each participant visualizes himself or herself as the deity or hero he or she will be working with, and goes through all three steps of attunement to that deity or hero.

The essential difference, of course, is that each participant visualizes and experiences the deity or hero as doing the polarity working, rather than leaving it on the human level. If Isis and Osiris are being evoked, the erotic and emotional attraction between the primary partners is not the core source of power in the working. Instead, the tremendous and eternal longing and love of Isis for Osiris and Osiris for Isis drives the magic. In a four-person working with the same focus, the secondary partners would embody two other gods or goddesses who are part of the same cycle of myths, and those deities will then maintain with their own divine powers the sacred space in which the love of Isis and Osiris is made manifest.

It is crucial in this form of working that the erotic and romantic attraction between the human participants should be raised up into, and absorbed by, their divine equivalents, rather than having the divine passion and love descend to the human level. If this latter happens, it can be extremely difficult for the humans in question to avoid being drawn into a romantic and sexual relationship, resulting in the failure of the polarity working. The key to avoiding this is for the participants to empty themselves of everything but an awareness of the divine presence. The Christian prayer "not my will, but Thine be done" captures something of the flavor of this state of consciousness, which might accordingly be phrased "not my love and desire, but Thine be expressed."

Close attention to releasing all remaining energy into the partner in the closing stages of the work, and letting go of the godform or hero form as completely as possible afterwards, are both worth doing to avoid problems with the overflow of divine energies into the human level. It is also wise for each participant in the working to have some outlet for ordinary sexual passion, so that if the polarity working does not succeed in releasing all the energies awakened in it, those energies can be earthed out in the time-honored way.

Solar current workings

The other form of advanced polarity working discussed in this book calls on the vertical polarities discussed in Chapter 5 of this book. The solar and telluric currents, the great patterns of magical force that surge respectively down from the sun and up from the center of the earth, can be drawn on in polarity workings. The two currents have their own distinctive characters and vary depending on time in the case of the solar current and place in the case of the telluric current.

For these reasons it is best to begin by working with them one at a time, and combine them in a single working once you are familiar with each current by itself.

The influence of time on the solar current is complex. The simplest way to track its cycles is to remember that dawn and noon are times of day when the solar current is strong, the moon's first quarter and the full moon have a similar role in the lunar month, and the spring equinox and the summer solstice are the equivalent times in the year. In each case there is a certain amount of room for variation. I have found that a working can begin up to half an hour before or after dawn or noon and still have full effect; six hours before or after the moment of first quarter or full moon seems to work well, and tradition in many schools of ceremonial magic has it that workings for solstices and equinoxes can be done any time up to forty-eight hours before or after the time the sun enters its new sign.

A more precise mode of timing the solar current makes use of the traditional planetary hours. These are not the same as the hours shown on a clock; the planetary hours of the day are twelve equal divisions of the time between sunrise and sunset, and the planetary hours of the night are twelve equal divisions of the time between sunset and sunrise. Because the length of day and night vary over the course of the year, they are only equal to an ordinary hour on two days a year, at the equinoxes. On other days they vary, and they also differ considerably in length depending on how far north or south of the equator you happen to be.

Each day is traditionally assigned to one of the seven classical planets, and each hour is likewise assigned to one of the same seven planets, as shown on the Planetary Hours tables given below. You can work out the hours for any day or night quite readily by looking up in a newspaper, almanac, or website, the time of sunrise and sunset in the place where you are. Calculate the number of hours and minutes between sunrise and sunset for the day, or between sunset and sunrise for the night; multiply the number of hours by 60 and add the number of minutes to get a total in minutes; divide by twelve, and that gets you the length in minutes for each planetary hour of the day or night. If you don't want to go to the trouble of doing all this, of course, there are also websites and phone apps that will calculate the planetary hours for you.

Planetary Hours of the Day

Hour	Sunday	Monday	Tuesday	Wednesday	Thursday	Friday	Saturday
1	Sun	Moon	Mars	Mercury	Jupiter	Venus	Saturn
2	Venus	Saturn	Sun	Moon	Mars	Mercury	Jupiter
3	Mercury	Jupiter	Venus	Saturn	Sun	Moon	Mars
4	Moon	Mars	Mercury	Jupiter	Venus	Saturn	Sun
5	Saturn	Sun	Moon	Mars	Mercury	Jupiter	Venus
6	Jupiter	Venus	Saturn	Sun	Moon	Mars	Mercury
7	Mars	Mercury	Jupiter	Venus	Saturn	Sun	Moon
8	Sun	Moon	Mars	Mercury	Jupiter	Venus	Saturn
9	Venus	Saturn	Sun	Moon	Mars	Mercury	Jupiter
10	Mercury	Jupiter	Venus	Saturn	Sun	Moon	Mars
11	Moon	Mars	Mercury	Jupiter	Venus	Saturn	Sun
12	Saturn	Sun	Moon	Mars	Mercury	Jupiter	Venus

Planetary Hours of the Night

Hour	Sunday	Monday	Tuesday	Wednesday	Thursday	Friday	Saturday
1	Jupiter	Venus	Saturn	Sun	Moon	Mars	
2	Mars	Mercury	Jupiter	Venus	Saturn	Sun	
3	Sun	Moon	Mars	Mercury	Jupiter	Venus	
4	Venus	Saturn	Sun	Moon	Mars	Mercury	
5	Mercury	Jupiter	Venus	Saturn	Sun	Moon	
6	Moon	Mars	Mercury	Jupiter	Venus	Saturn	
7	Saturn	Sun	Moon	Mars	Mercury	Jupiter	
8	Jupiter	Venus	Saturn	Sun	Moon	Mars	
9	Mars	Mercury	Jupiter	Venus	Saturn	Sun	
10	Sun	Moon	Mars	Mercury	Jupiter	Venus	
11	Venus	Saturn	Sun	Moon	Mars	Mercury	
12	Mercury	Jupiter	Venus	Saturn	Sun	Moon	

The key to using the planetary hours for timing workings with the solar current is that the hour of any planet, on the day of that planet, gives you a relatively pure flow of energy. Mages traditionally use these times to consecrate planetary talismans or invoke planetary spirits, but the same times can be used for polarity workings. For general purposes, the day and hour of the Sun is the best time for solar current workings, and the day and hour of Jupiter or of Venus is nearly as good. The days and hours of Mercury and the Moon tend to have very unstable energy flows and should be used for solar current workings only after plenty of experience has been gained at less challenging times. The days and hours of Mars and Saturn, the two malefic planets, should be left strictly alone except by experienced mages who have specific projects needing one or the other of these difficult energies.

At the upper end of complexity in terms of timing the solar current is the art of electional astrology. This allows the mage to choose a time for an event when the entire pattern of the heavens is favorable for the event. Doing this effectively requires a solid background in general astrological studies as well as a working knowledge of the specifics of electional astrology. Two books, *Electional Astrology* by Vivian Robson and *Secrets of Planetary Magic* by Christopher Warnock, are useful guides to students, but these have to be combined with plenty of study and practice to reach the level of skill at which times for solar current workings can be selected.

Telluric current workings

The telluric current, by contrast, responds to place rather than time, and this imposes its own set of constraints on the practitioner. To begin with, the Western occult traditions have preserved much less about the magical properties of place than about those of time. It's possible to use Asian traditions such as feng-shui, the Chinese art of place divination, to identify a suitable place for telluric current workings, but this requires as much study and practice as learning electional astrology. A handful of Western occultists, most notably Nigel Pennick, have worked at rebuilding comparable European traditions from the surviving fragments. Their work can be used as a way to make sense of the magical properties of place, but this also requires extensive study and practice.

A simpler method, comparable to the first two timing options for the solar current mentioned above, is the use of dowsing. This depends to some extent on personal talent, but many people can learn to dowse readily from the many books available on the subject. Pendulum dowsing tends to be more useful for this kind of work than the classic forked hazel stick, since dowsing over a map is easier for most people when a pendulum is used. This allows you to search through an entire region without needing to go through it step by step on foot.

Except in very advanced forms of work, your goal in this mode of dowsing is simply to find an area where the telluric current is clean and strong. Once you have chosen a general location, practical concerns such as the need for a private space for ritual can join with dowsing methods to find the best possible location for the working. Only when you have a good sense of the magical and energetic properties of different places is it worth choosing a place specifically for the quality of telluric current that rises there. This is experimental work and your own perceptions and experiences will have to guide you.

It is sometimes possible to do workings of this kind in an ancient holy place. Be very careful before attempting this, however. First, different holy places have different energies, and not all of them are suitable for any given kind of magical working. Second, some holy places can manifest a level of power that few if any mages today are capable of handling safely. Third, many holy places are protected by spiritual guardians, who may not look kindly on your attempts to make use of the powers of the place. For these reasons, telluric current work with holy places should be left to very experienced mages, and the working should be tested out in some safer place repeatedly before any attempt is made to draw on the energies of a holy place.

Working the vertical polarity

The method for working with the solar or telluric currents, or both of them together, follows the same pattern as the basic workings given in Chapter 6. There are two main differences. The first, of course, is that the working takes place at a time chosen with regard to the solar current, a place chosen with regard to the telluric current, or both.

The second difference comes in after the fifth step of either the two-person or four-person version, right after the formation of the energy link from solar plexus to solar plexus. Once that link is well established, for a solar current working, one partner begins to draw down the solar current from high above through the crown of his head and down the midline of his body to the solar plexus, and send it across to the solar plexus of the other partner. The other partner receives the energy and sends it back up the midline of her body to the crown of her head and then up high into the heavens.

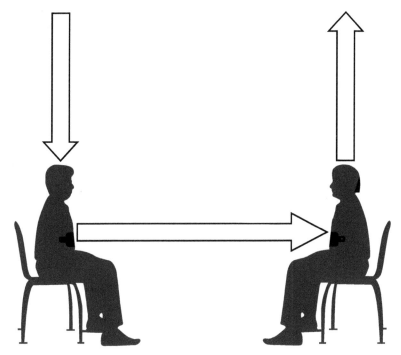

Movement of the solar curent in advanced workings.

Working the solar current

The pronouns just used are of course deliberate. Much more often than not, if the partnership is between a man and a woman, for reasons covered in an earlier chapter, the man will find it easier to bring the solar current down and the woman will find it easier to receive the solar current and send it back up. Same-sex or intersex couples will need to experiment to see which of them is best suited to each of these roles.

For a telluric current working, immediately after the fifth step of the working given earlier, one partner begins to draw up the telluric current from the center of the earth through her perineum (the space between the genitals and the anus) and up the midline of her body to the solar plexus, and send it across to the solar plexus of the other partner. The other partner receives the energy and sends it back down the midline of his body to his perineum and then back down to the center of the earth. Once again, the choice of pronouns here is deliberate, since women tend to better at bringing up the telluric current and men at sending it back down again to its source.

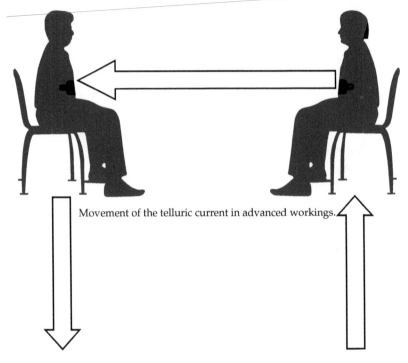

Movement of the telluric current in advanced workings.

Working the telluric current

In either case, once the solar or telluric current has been brought into play, the rest of the working follows one of the patterns set out in Chapter 6, depending on what kind of working you and your partner have in mind. Take your time establishing the current and feeling it flow through you, and proceed to the next step of the working only when both partners are ready—some simple wordless signal such as a nod can be arranged in advance to allow each partner to tell the other that they are ready.

The first time you work with either of these patterns, even if you do it at a suitable time (for the solar current) or a suitable place (for the telluric current), the effects will likely be modest at best. It takes practice to get any significant effect at all. Polarity partners who work with one of the two currents systematically will develop the ability to raise considerable amounts of power that way, but "systematically" is the operative word.

Reinforcing that work with a daily exercise that links into the same current—for example, the Golden Dawn tradition's Middle Pillar exercise, which works with the solar current—will speed up the process considerably.[29] If you and your polarity partner practice such an exercise regularly and have a year or more of experience with it, it is also possible to incorporate the exercise directly into the polarity working. Using the Middle Pillar exercise as an example, right after the fifth step of the working, both partners perform that exercise together, awakening the five centers of the Middle Pillar in the usual way while seated. Once both have completed the exercise, the solar current is brought into play as described above. This can bring through a great deal of additional power.

The centers of the Middle Pillar exercise awakened in the two partners.

Middle Pillar exercise

Is it possible to work with both currents in a single working? Yes, but this takes ample practice and a fair amount of skill. To do this, at the appropriate point in the working, the partners establish one current, and once it is firmly in place, they establish the other current. Thereafter each of the primary partners has to keep bringing one current into the working, and keep sending the other current back to its source, while simultaneously managing the flows of energy between the partners and the work of the ceremony! This is not easy. Once it can be done reliably, however, it opens the way to workings of considerable power, and to the formulation of the third, lunar current, which has its own range of magical potentials.

One further step at the high end of complexity in polarity work is the combination of godform work with the solar and telluric currents.

---

[29] For this exercise, see Regardie 1945.

This obviously requires even more skill and practice than either method by itself. For this reason, no instructions will be given in this book on how to do it. If you and your partner do sufficient work with godforms or hero forms, on the one hand, and the solar and telluric currents on the other, it will be obvious to you how to combine them. If you have not yet done plenty of work with both these advanced methods, you have no business attempting to combine them.

Three advanced workings

To give advanced students of polarity magic templates on which to construct their own workings, I have included three examples below: a godform working of Osiris and Isis meant to empower a temple space for magical and spiritual workings; a hero form working of Robin Hood and Maid Marian to awaken the spirit of liberty in a community or nation; and a combined solar and telluric working to formulate the lunar current to further the spiritual development of the participants.

The ritual of Osiris and Isis

This working requires eight people: the primary partners, who will take on the godforms of Osiris and Isis; the secondary partners, who will take on the godforms of Horus and Hathor; and four additional participants, who will take on the godforms of the four Canopic gods, Amesheth, Duamutef, Kebsenuf, and Hapi.[30] All participants should be competent practitioners of the general system of magic used in the working. The primary and secondary partners need to have considerable experience in polarity magic; the other four participants need not have this background, but should be able to visualize a godform clearly and maintain it for the duration of a ritual, while also moving energy and assisting the other participants with their visualizations. All of the participants should be familiar with the Egyptian myths of Isis and Osiris.

A standard text such as E.A. Wallis Budge's *The Gods of the Egyptians* should be consulted to get the details of each of the godforms. The Egyptians were very precise about the images of their gods and

---

[30] Those readers who work with the Golden Dawn system may find it useful to know that in the original papers of that order, and later works based on them such as Israel Regardie's *The Golden Dawn*, these names are given the spellings they were assigned in nineteenth-century scholarship: Ameshet, Tmoumathph, Kabexnuv, and Ahephi.

goddesses, and this makes those images unusually effective in any form of magic that uses godforms—provided, of course, that the traditional details are visualized exactly. In this working the forms of Osiris and Isis to use are seated in thrones, and the forms of Horus and Hathor to use are standing; all four of these godforms have empty hands. The forms of the four Canopic gods to use are mummified, with only the head visible above the mummy-wrappings.

Each participant needs to memorize the godform he or she will be taking on in the working, and practice taking on the godform until that process can be completed promptly without any detail being left out. Each member of the primary and secondary partnerships must also memorize the godform taken by the person with whom he or she will be in polarity relationship in the working—thus, the mage who will be taking on the godform of Osiris should also memorize the form of Isis, and vice versa, and the mage who will be taking on the godform of Horus should also memorize the form of Hathor, and vice versa. The four mages who will be taking on the forms of the Canopic gods should also memorize the forms of Osiris and Isis.

Finally, it is helpful for the participants to practice taking on their god-forms together. To do this, have everyone present and in the position they will occupy during the working. Perform whatever opening cere-mony will be used in the ritual. Once everyone is seated again, the mage who will be taking on the form of Isis recites the invocation of the gods and goddesses mentioned in the second step below, and all present then go on to the third step given below, in which each participant recites a silent invocation and then takes on the godform. Hold the godforms in place for a short time, then go directly to the twelfth step below, release the godforms, thank the gods and goddesses, and perform the closing ceremony. If the participants have not worked together before, it will be helpful to do this several times before proceeding to the working itself.

The ritual is performed as follows.

First, open the temple in the usual fashion, using whatever ceremo-nial opening is appropriate to the tradition in which the working is being done.

Second, the mage who will be taking on the godform of Osiris pro-claims the purpose of the working—to empower the temple space so that all future magical and spiritual workings performed in it will be strengthened by the power and presence of the gods. The mage who will be taking on the godform of Isis then recites an invocation of the gods and goddesses whose forms will be invoked in the working, asking them to direct their presence and power to fulfill the purpose of the ritual. All participants concentrate on the words as they are spoken.

Third, each participant silently recites an invocation to the god or goddess whose form he or she will take on, makes contact with the deity, and then formulates the godform. A silent signal, such as turning the palms of the hands upwards, is given by each participant once the godform has been taken on. From this point until the twelfth step given below, the godforms rather than the human participants will perform all the ritual actions in the working. The role of the human mages is limited to establishing the imaginative forms through which the power and passion of the deities becomes manifest. The mages working with the godforms of Osiris, Isis, Horus, and Hathor make the same physical movements as their godforms—for example, raising their hands—but this is purely so that the inner movements of the working can be coordinated.

Fourth, the godforms of Isis and Osiris (and the mages who have taken on these godforms) raise their hands and make connection, palm to palm, as in the third section of the two- or four-person basic workings given in the previous chapter. Since they are deities, Isis and Osiris do not need to trace the elemental symbols on their hands before making a polarity connection. It is essential that the mages who have taken on these godforms have plenty of experience with that form of polarity connection, however, so that they can imagine the experience with clarity and force. At this time, all participants should begin contemplating the love of Osiris for Isis and of Isis for Osiris.

Fifth, once the palm connection between Osiris and Isis is well established, the godforms of Horus and Hathor (and the mages who have taken on these godforms) raise their hands to shoulder level, angled outward, as in the fourth step of the basic four-person form given in the previous chapter. The godforms of Isis and Osiris (and the mages who have taken on these godforms) then rotate their own palms outwards, releasing the palm to palm contact with each other and establishing it with Horus and Hathor. The diamond of polarity flow established by this process should be given ample time to strengthen and stabilize. Meanwhile, the four Canopic gods become aware of one another. They do not raise their hands, being wrapped like mummies, and the mages working with these godforms leave their hands down. The Canopic gods still form a square of energies that contains the diamond of forces and adds stability to the working. This is visualized intently by the four mages who have taken on the forms of the Canopic gods.

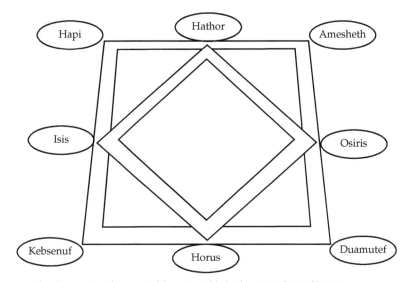

The diamond and square of forces established among the godforms.

Diamond and square of forces

Sixth, the godforms of Osiris and Isis establish between them the main current of polarity from solar plexus to solar plexus. This current carries the full force of the love and longing of Isis and Osiris for each other, and it should be given ample time to build in strength until it holds as much polarity energy as the mages in the working can handle.

Seventh, from the godforms of Osiris and Isis, a second beam or current of energy streams up from the solar plexus at an angle to a point above and midway between them. Where the two currents meet above they form an image of the sun, which radiates light and warmth down on both participants and on the entire working space. Once the sun has been established, the love and erotic tension between Isis and Osiris streams up into the sun. All the human participants in the working, while maintaining their own energy patterns, imagine this flow as intensely as they can. Let the sun become the focus of a sense of steadily building pressure, like the pressure of erotic energy moving toward orgasm. Maintain the sense of rising pressure as long as possible, so that the working reaches its highest potential of power.

Eighth, the mage who has taken on the godform of Osiris speaks, repeating the intention of the working; he does this not as himself but as Osiris. When he has finished, the mage who has taken on the godform of Isis repeats the same intention, speaking as Isis. Thereafter the mages who have taken on the godforms of Horus and Hathor do the same thing, one after the other. Then, at a signal from Isis, the energy that has built up in the image of the sun is allowed to discharge straight down into the temple space in a single intense ray of force. This visualization should also be maintained for some time, as not all the power will descend at once. Let it all complete its descent before finishing.

Ninth, the mage who has taken on the godform of Hathor, speaking as the goddess, says, "It is accomplished." This is repeated in turn by the mages who have taken the forms of Horus, Isis, and Osiris, in that order.

Tenth, the godforms of Osiris and Isis dissolve the image of the sun overhead and the two currents of force rising to it. They focus for a short time on the contact from solar plexus to solar plexus established in the sixth step, releasing all erotic and romantic energy in the process, while Horus and Hathor maintain the diamond established in the fifth step and the Canopic gods maintain the surrounding square.

Eleventh, the godforms of Osiris and Isis release the current uniting solar plexus to solar plexus. They (and the mages who have taken on these godforms) move their hands inward, and reconnect from palm to palm. At this point the godforms of Horus and Hathor release the diamond of forces and they, and the mages working with them, lower their hands. The Canopic gods release the square of forces at the same time.

Twelfth, the godforms of Osiris and Isis release the connection from palm to palm and, along with the mages working these forms, lower their hands. This is the signal for each of the participants to repeat silently a prayer of thanks to the god or goddess whose form they have taken, and to release the godform. A silent signal, such as turning the palms of the hands upwards, is given by each participant once the godform has been released. Once this is done, the closing ceremony is performed to complete the working.

The ritual of Robin Hood and Maid Marian

This working requires at least four people and can be done with any larger number, provided that everyone who is present has enough basic magical training that they can assist the working rather than detracting from it. Its intention is to awaken the spirit of liberty in a country or a community that has lost that spirit in its daily affairs. This should be done only after ample reflection, and divination should be consulted to be sure the ritual is appropriate. Everyone involved should keep in mind that the spirit of liberty will not necessarily inspire everyone in a country or community to behave in ways that the participants in the ritual would approve!

In this working the primary couple, who must be experienced polarity mages, take on the hero forms of Robin Hood and Maid Marian. The secondary couple, who should have some experience in polarity magic, take on the hero forms of Little John and Friar Tuck, and the other participants take on the forms of Robin Hood's merry men and the ladies of the greenwood. All the participants should be thoroughly familiar with the legends of Robin Hood in their medieval and modern forms. Reading material can be circulated among the members of the group, and a video night for the entire group beforehand featuring *The Adventures of Robin Hood*—the classic 1938 film version starring Errol Flynn and Olivia de Havilland—might be another good way to help this process along.

All participants should spend sufficient time learning to take on the hero forms they will be using in the working. This is as true of the merry men and ladies as it is of the primary and secondary couples. Each participant should spend time daily in the week before the working building up an imaginary form dressed in the traditional garments assigned by the legends, and meditating on the experience of living in the greenwood as an outlaw, free from the oppression of an unjust system but constantly at risk from weather, wild beasts, and the Sheriff of Nottingham's men. Some form of costume should be provided for the working itself; this can be as simple as a hip-length green tabard or as complex as medieval costume in Lincoln green, depending on the resources available to the group.

Once everyone has practiced taking on their hero forms and is familiar with the ritual and the legend of Robin Hood, the ritual can be performed. It is done as follows.

First, open the temple in the usual fashion, using whatever ceremonial opening is appropriate to the tradition in which the working is being done.

Second, all participants enter into meditation using whatever method is provided by the tradition being worked. The mages who will be taking on the forms of Robin Hood and Maid Marian then lead the entire group in a guided meditation. All participants should visualize the scenes being described as vividly as possible as the following words are spoken.

Robin Hood – "Come with me into the greenwood. Leave behind everything that belongs to the outer world, just as the outlaws of old left behind everything when they fled to the depths of Sherwood Forest."

Maid Marian – "Come with me into the greenwood. Seek the shelter of this place between the worlds, just as the outlaws of old sought the shelter of the woodland in their quest for freedom from oppression."

Robin Hood – "Come with me into the greenwood. Before us the great oaks rise tall, and beneath them the brush presses thick. At first glance we see no way through the barrier of boughs and branches and leaves they raise against us."

Maid Marian – "Come with me into the greenwood. Take another look, and a narrow path hidden under the oaks leads through the thickets into the heart of the forest. We follow that path, knowing that the enemies of liberty cannot find it."

Robin Hood – "Come with me into the greenwood. Sun dapples the ground, streaming past the leaves of the mighty oaks. A great stag in the middle distance sees us and bounds away, vanishing into the forest. Birds sing unseen in the branches overhead, and a wind rustles the leaves as it passes."

Maid Marian – "Come with me into the greenwood. In the heart of the forest we find a clearing, and in the clearing is a circle of logs laid out as a place for us to sit. Around the logs the grass grows green, and the sky above is blue where it shows through the oak leaves. We are safe here and our work awaits."

Robin Hood and Maid Marian together – "Come with us into the greenwood."

Third, all participants take on their hero forms. Ample time should be provided for this purpose. Each person, as well as imagining their own forms, imagines those around them in comparable forms, and reinforces the framing image of a clearing in the greenwood surrounding the entire group. A silent signal, such as folding the hands together in the lap, is given by each person once his or her form is in place.

Fourth, the following dialogue takes place between the mages who have taken the forms of Robin Hood and Maid Marian:

Robin Hood – "The intention of our work is to awaken the spirit of liberty in (name of country or place)."

Maid Marian – "As you seek liberty for yourself, will you grant it to all others?"

Robin Hood – "Yes, I will."

A similar dialogue is repeated between the mages who have taken the forms of Little John and Friar Tuck:

Little John – "It is time to awaken the spirit of liberty in (name of country or place)."

Friar Tuck – "As you seek liberty for yourself, will you grant it to all others?"

Little John – "Yes, I will."

A third dialogue includes everyone present:

Robin Hood – "Let each and all of us join our strength together to awaken the spirit of liberty in (name of country or place)."

Maid Marian – "Merry men and ladies of the greenwood, as you seek liberty for yourself, will you grant it to all others?"

Everyone present – "Yes, we will."

Robin Hood – "Then let the work begin."

Fifth, the work proceeds as in the basic four-person method described in Chapter 6: the forms of Robin Hood and Maid Marian trace the elemental symbols on their hands and make contact from palm to palm, then the forms of Little John and Friar Tuck trace the elemental symbols on their hands and form the diamond of forces with the primary couple, and the primary couple formulates the upright equilateral triangle with the sun at its uppermost point. All of this work is visualized as being performed by the hero forms rather than by the mages themselves.

While this is going on, all the participants who are erotically attracted to women focus their attention on Maid Marian—not on the mage who has taken on that form, but on the hero form itself—imagining Maid Marian as supremely beautiful and desirable. At the same time, all the participants who are erotically attracted to men focus their attention on Robin Hood—again, the form rather than the mage who has taken it on—imagining Robin Hood as supremely handsome and desirable. This helps build the polarity between the primary partners and will strengthen the working considerably.

Sixth, when the sun at the peak of the triangle is fully charged with erotic energy, Robin Hood says aloud, "Behold the Sun of Liberty!" This is repeated by Maid Marian, Little John, and Friar Tuck, one at a time, and then the whole group says at once, "Behold the Sun of Liberty!" At that moment the energy of the sun is allowed to discharge itself into the ground, assisted by the visualizations of all present. This process should be sustained until all the energy has discharged itself, which should take some time. Meanwhile, the participants should imagine the energy thus released flowing out to fill the entire geographical area that is meant to be influenced, filling it with the spirit of liberty and influencing all its inhabitants with that spirit.

Seventh, when the energy is fully transferred to the land, the image of the sun and the two currents rising toward it is dissolved. The structure of energy channels built up in the fifth step is taken down stage by stage, as in the seventh, eighth, and ninth steps of the basic four-person working given in the previous chapter.

Eighth, at a silent signal from the mage who has taken on the form of Robin Hood, all participants in the working release their hero forms. Once this is complete, the mage who worked with the form of

Friar Tuck thanks the spiritual influences that have been called on during the working. The closing ceremony used by the tradition in which the working is done is then performed.

The ritual of the lunar current

This ritual is best done with two people, and is presented below in that form, though it can also be done with four or more. All the participants should be experienced polarity mages; they should also be experienced in a system of magic or occult training that works with both the solar and telluric currents—for example, the methods taught in my books *The Druid Magic Handbook, The Dolmen Arch,* and *The Way of the Golden Section.* Finally, they should both have done polarity work with the solar current by itself, and with the telluric current by itself, using the methods described earlier in this chapter. Similar workings can be designed for the solar current alone, or for the telluric current alone, but readers who practice a system of magic that uses only one current will need to devise a working suited to the needs of that system.

When the solar and telluric currents are both invoked, time and place both need to be taken into account. The methods for doing so, as given earlier in this chapter, can be applied in as simple or complex a form as possible. It is quite effective to do this working at dawn or noon in a place that has been identified as suitable by simple pendulum dowsing. More demanding choices—for example, electing a time using astrological means and doing the working in an ancient holy place of suitable type—can potentially call up levels of power that are dangerous for less experienced mages to work with. Do the simpler approach first before trying the more complex methods; this will keep you from getting over your head too quickly.

The requirements of the ritual are those of the basic two-person form given in the previous chapter. The ritual is performed as follows.

First, proceed with the basic two-person working from the beginning as far as the end of the fifth step.

Second, once the contact from solar plexus to solar plexus has been well established, bring through the solar current as described earlier in this chapter. The solar current should descend through one of the partners as far as the solar plexus, cross to the other partner, and rise up through the other partner into the heavens. Allow ample time to get this current established and stable.

Third, bring through the telluric current as described earlier in this chapter. The telluric current should rise up through one of the partners to solar plexus level, cross to the other partner, and descend through the other partner into the heart of the earth. Note that each partner should draw in one current from above or below, and release the other current to above or below, as shown in the accompanying diagram. Note also that the two currents should be felt as occupying slightly different positions in the flow from solar plexus to solar plexus; the solar current should be slightly above the telluric current, as though the two are sliding smoothly past each other as they move in opposite directions. Maintaining these two currents as steady and balanced flows is tricky, and so both participants should be sure they have the currents stable before continuing.

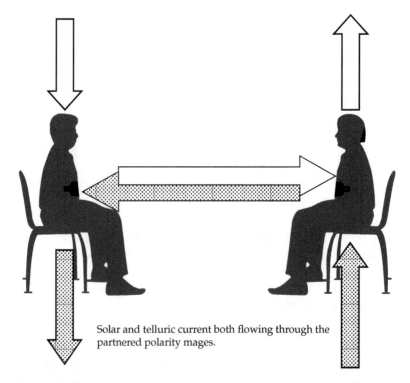

Solar and telluric current both flowing through the partnered polarity mages.

Solar and telluric currents

Fourth, when the currents are stable, both participants bring the two currents together: the flow of the solar current from solar plexus to solar plexus shifts slightly downward and the corresponding flow of the telluric current shifts slightly upward, so that the two flows occupy the same space. As this is done, midway between the two participants, a blaze of pure white light is born, as shown in the diagram below. The white light streams outward in all directions, illuminating both participants.

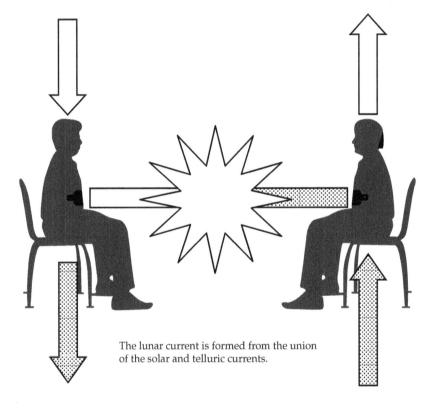

The lunar current is formed from the union of the solar and telluric currents.

Lunar current

Fifth, after this has been maintained for a time, the blaze of white light is divided in half, and one half moves to the solar plexus of each participant. What happens next depends entirely on the system of magical practice the participants use. If that system includes a practice that awakens energy centers inside the subtle body, the blaze of white light is guided from the solar plexus to each of those centers—for example, readers who are working with the Grail Working taught in my books *The Druid Magic Handbook* and *The Dolmen Arch* may direct it from the solar plexus into the three Cauldrons, beginning with the lowest Cauldron and ascending from there, while readers who use the method given for initiates in *The Way of the Golden Section* will find it helpful to stabilize the light in the solar plexus and then send a current up the vagus nerve to the pineal gland. This visualization is sustained for as long as both participants choose.

Sixth, both participants allow the light in the centers within the bodies to fade from immediate awareness. Then they allow the flow of the telluric current to close down, followed by the solar current.

Seventh, the working is closed down as in the seventh, eighth, and ninth steps of the basic two-person form.

Other advanced workings

The three advanced workings given in this chapter should be treated as examples to spark your own imagination rather than as endpoints beyond which no further advance is possible. Each of the workings given here, to begin with, can be modified freely to focus on different intentions and purposes, and they can also be used as templates for workings that use different godforms, hero forms, or energy currents. Once a pair or group of polarity mages have mastered the basic methods, explored their practical applications, and proceeded to work with godforms, hero forms, and the various energies of the macrocosm, the possibilities for advanced polarity workings are all but limitless. The system of magic you practice and the approach to occult philosophy that undergirds that system should be taken as a source of ideas for further development.

Just as every mage who gets past the basics of the magical art will develop a personal style of working, every working couple or group of polarity mages will develop a style unique to themselves. The few records of earlier explorations of polarity magic that are available to occultists today, such as Alan Richardson's valuable volume *Dancers to the Gods*, are among other things chronicles of the development of such a style, and of course they can also be used as a valuable source of inspiration for mages who choose to do so.

CHAPTER 8

Mass polarity magic

S o far the workings discussed in this book have been on the intimate scale of two or four people, or the slightly less intimate space of a magical lodge or working group. This is intentional. Most effective magical work is done in such settings, or in the disciplined solitude of a mage practicing alone. Most polarity magic follows that rule.

It is possible, however, to do polarity workings on a much larger scale, with large crowds of people involved. Such large-scale mass polarity workings take place quite often in today's society. It's simply that very few people recognize them for what they are, and even fewer understand that they can be used—and are more than occasionally used—for magical purposes.

One of the best places to watch polarity in action, in fact, is at a good rock concert. Up on stage is the star, dressed in an erotically alluring outfit, moving his or her body sexually to music that is backed by a powerful hypnotic beat. The other participants on stage are there to maintain the musical incantation and, from time to time, take over the lead so the star doesn't burn out completely from the raw intensity of the energies being channeled. The other side of the polarity working? That is provided by the audience: shrieking, moaning, swaying to the beat of the music, and pouring out etheric energy toward the star, in response to the torrent of astral stimulation he or she gives them. When a rock concert really hits its stride, the energy volleys back and forth from the star to the audience and back again, transforming the band and the audience alike into a single organism intoxicated by sheer libido.

The same process put to different uses can be seen in action at a church service where the clergy know how to work with energy. These days, for reasons we will discuss a little later in this chapter, that is less common than it should be; this is why so many church services every Sunday are so dull and so ineffectual. Go to an African-American church where the minister has learned how to shape and direct the energy of the crowd, on the other hand, and you'll see polarity magic handled very capably indeed. Energies surge back and forth from minister to congregation in the call and response of the sermon, just as they do when the rock concert finds its rhythm, but the goal isn't simply to have a good time. If, as Dion Fortune suggested, magic is the art and science of causing changes in consciousness in accordance with will, a church service of the kind just described, is potent magic, directed toward the states of consciousness described in Christian scriptures as faith, hope, and charity.

A much quieter but equally intense play of energies can be witnessed in those churches that practice the traditional sacraments and haven't allowed those potent ceremonial workings to be turned into empty formalities by ill-considered modernizations. There the flow of power doesn't involve loud noises and swaying bodies. Instead, rapt attention from a still and focused congregation, many of them caught up in silent prayer, sends energies streaming toward the altar, where the priest recites the archaic worlds of a ritual two millennia old. When the ceremony of communion is done by a priest and a congregation that know their inward and outward roles by heart, the words "This is My Body" send a shockwave through the stillness that lands with the force of a gut punch. It's not surprising that genuine miracles happen in such a setting.

One more example will finish making the point, and hint at the power and some of the perils of this mode of polarity working. The scene? A rundown auditorium in a working-class neighborhood somewhere in Germany in 1930. The podium has a swastika banner draped over it and another has been hoisted up onto the wall behind it. Into the auditorium streams a crowd of ordinary Germans, frightened and shaken by the chaotic aftermath of defeat in the First World War and a decade of brutal economic crisis.

The first three rows, however, are set aside for a very particular kind of attendee. The uniformed guards who serve as ushers, low-ranking members of the SS, call them "the varicose veins brigade," and make coarse jokes about them. The guards are not initiates. All they know is that their Führer has instructed them to fill those rows with middle-aged women who come to the meeting unaccompanied by men.

The crowd settles down, and Adolf Hitler comes to the podium. At the beginning of his speech he seems shy and fumbling, but that passes off quickly as the flow of polarity that links him with the sexually unfulfilled women in the front rows begins to build. Within a few minutes he has slipped into what witnesses at the time described as a mediumistic trance, and the unspoken passions and hatreds of his audience stream together into a torrent of force that Hitler, a highly competent mage, knows exactly how to put to work. By the time the speech is half over, even an audience that started out skeptical is wailing, shrieking, sobbing, and cheering on cue. When the speech is over, some of them will join the Nazi Party and many more will vote for Hitler in the upcoming elections.

From many to one

Mass polarity workings, as these examples suggest, typically involve an exchange of polarity between one person who knows how to direct energies, and a crowd whose members have energy to offer. The degree to which the working is overtly sexual in nature varies from one case to another. Rock concerts generally have quite a bit of flagrantly erotic content, from the suggestive clothes so many stars wear on stage to the even more suggestive rhythms of movements and music, while the erotic dimension of the communion ceremony is tastefully veiled in symbolic forms: the phallic cross, the vaginal chalice, and the rest of it. Yet the same energies that flow back and forth in a polarity working of the kind described in the previous two chapters also move between the audience and the person at the center of its attention in mass polarity workings.

Rock concerts and the other examples of mass polarity workings differ in another respect, of course. A rock concert has no purpose other than entertainment, and the exchange of energy between performer and audience is normally allowed to ground out afterwards in sex: thus the legendary erotic antics of so many rock performers backstage and in their private lives more generally, and the intensely sexual ambience of rock music in popular culture. The church services have another purpose, though they can readily do the same thing as a rock concert if their energy is mishandled—a point that we will discuss at length further on in this chapter.

The final example also had another purpose, of course. Adolf Hitler was far too capable a mage to allow the energy he evoked to be wasted on erotic behavior. The astral charge that gave the Nazi Party its power over human minds, and still gives its symbols extraordinary emotional force most of a century after Hitler's death, came from the mass polarity workings Hitler and his inner circle of occultists arranged and carried out: first on the small scale described above when Hitler was still an outsider clawing his way up the ladder to power, then on the grand scale once the Nazi Party seized power and all the resources of the German state could be put to use in the vast annual rallies at Nuremberg. Leni Riefenstahl's infamous propaganda film *Triumph of the Will*, which chronicled the 1934 rally, gives an uncomfortably clear view of the kinds of magical working performed at these events.

There are significant practical differences between mass polarity workings of the kind discussed in this chapter and the smaller-scale workings discussed in previous chapters. The most important of these differences should be obvious from the examples given above. In a mass polarity working, the members of the crowd who are providing energy to the working do not need to know anything about magic. They may not even recognize that anything magical is going on. The lack of magical training and shared intention limits the amount of energy any one member of the audience can provide, but this limitation can be outweighed by sheer numbers. A thousand people at a rock concert caught up in the music can provide much more energy than any one polarity mage, however well trained.

The more people are in the audience, the more intense the energies that are aroused. The less they know about magic, the more competent the mage who is the center of their attention therefore has to be. Strictly speaking, magical training is not necessary to provide the necessary level of competence. Plenty of musicians and ministers figure out how to work with the energy of a crowd by trial and error—though it's no accident that so many popular music stars of the last three quarters of a century have dabbled, or more than dabbled, in occultism, and I suspect quite a bit of working knowledge of occult practice is passed on secretly among ministers too. A good basic grounding in practical magic makes it much easier to work with the energy flows in mass polarity workings, however, and also makes it easier to avoid the dangers of this mode of magical work.

What are these dangers? One of the most obvious, and also one of the most common, can be seen in action in the kind of bland, tired church service where it feels as though everyone present would much rather be somewhere else. The minister reads a sermon, and though it may stir some emotional reactions here and there in the crowd, the energy falters and fades away almost as quickly as it appears. The music of the choir may be technically good but no one gets caught up in it. Any ritual actions that might be part of the service fail to reach the deep levels of the mind where symbolism is a potent force. Once the ceremony is over, everyone sighs with relief at the completion of a dull but necessary chore, and troops downstairs for weak coffee and stale cookies before leaving for another week.

What has happened here? It's more relevant to ask what hasn't happened here, and the answer is simple: no polarity flow has taken place between the minister and his congregation. The imaginations and emotions of the congregation have not been stirred, the life force has not been roused, and so no currents of astral and etheric energy have empowered the service and made miracles possible. To be fair, some people prefer services of this kind. Spending a Sunday morning this way is safe, it's predictable, and there is not the slightest risk that the divine presence will show up and disrupt the proceedings. Jesus of Nazareth had a similar type in mind when he said, "They have their reward."[31]

Then there is the other kind of failure, which has spawned gaudy headlines for decades now. Again, church services make a good example, but in this case the kind to watch is one that seems almost too successful. The imaginations and emotions of the congregation are stirred into motion by the music and words of the service, all eyes are fixed on the minister, the energy flows freely back and forth. The problem doesn't become apparent until after the service, and then the downside is clear only if you happen to know that the minister is having hot sex with the organist when he isn't bedding any one of five or

---

[31] Matthew 6:2.

six neglected spouses, or getting rather too friendly with the kids who attend Sunday school.

Nor is the congregation exempt from the same sorts of misbehavior. Behind closed doors, a great deal of sex is taking place, most of it without the least reference to marriage vows or the sexual teachings of the church in question. Sometimes things stabilize at that level and everyone goes on for years at a time, wrestling unsuccessfully with desires they can't admit in public, and pretending to everyone else that nothing is wrong. At least as often, however the erotic pressure builds within minister and congregation alike, until it finally blows up into open scandal. Tolerably often the scandal tears the church to shreds and drives many members of its congregation straight out of religion altogether.

The perils of mass polarity

Memoirs by people who have experienced this latter process in action often make highly educational reading for students of polarity magic. One of the best examples of this literature is *Don't Call Me Brother* by Austin Miles, a circus ringmaster who was recruited to the clergy by PTL Ministries, the church at the center of one of the most lurid religious scandals of the 1980s. Miles became a successful minister, then watched PTL Ministries blow itself sky-high in a welter of financial improprieties and wild sexual escapades, and left the ministry to resume his former profession for a while. (He later returned to the ministry and was still active in it at the time of his death in 2013, but as far as I know no further trace of scandal touched him.)

His memoir is colorful reading. It describes in unsparing detail the scandals that overwhelmed PTL and its leaders, Jim and Tammy Faye Bakker. In the process, Miles showed exactly how mishandled polarity led straight to some of the most embarrassing incidents in the organization's collapse. This is all the more intriguing in that Miles seems to have known nothing about occultism and apparently never heard of polarity magic.

As a professional showman, however, he knew how to draw and hold the attention of an audience, and he recognized the exact parallels between his job as a circus ringmaster and the work of a religious leader. He also watched the ministers at the core of PTL ministries get drawn into a vortex of sexual excess. He apparently did not recognize that these two things were linked together, but his account is detailed enough that anyone who knows what to look for can make the necessary connections.

What caused the mass polarity workings at PTL Ministries to spin out of control? For that matter, what has caused hundreds of equivalent scandals in countless other denominations in recent decades? The explanation is quite simple: over the course of the twentieth century, nearly all of the religious denominations in North America and western Europe stopped providing traditional modes of training for priests and ministers, and restructured seminaries to teach a standard liberal arts education instead.

The older model of clergy education focused on personal spiritual practice and mentorship by experienced working clergy, both of which offered opportunities for novice clergy to learn how to deal with the subtle side of religious worship. I have been told, though I cannot document this, that in at least some denominations there was quite a bit of oral instruction passed on to candidates for ordination which dealt explicitly with energy flows.

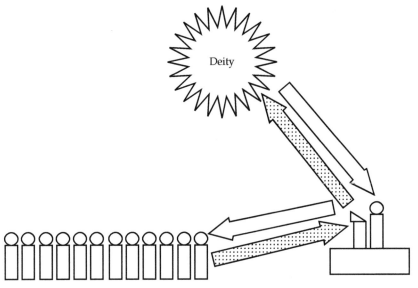

In an effective religious service, the minister gathers up the etheric force from the congregation and passes it on as an offering to the deity being worshipped, and sends back the astral current from the deity to the congregation.

An effective religious service

As a result, the congregational worship of an earlier time functioned as a polarity working with three poles: the congregation, the celebrant (the clergyperson performing the service), and the deity who was worshipped. The congregation provided etheric energy, which was gathered and offered up to the deity by the celebrant. The deity responded by sending down a current of astral blessing, which was received by the celebrant and sent on to the congregation. To make this pattern function effectively, the celebrant had to be a middleman, not a stopping point for either current of energy. Magical training makes this easy, but personal devotion to the deity and a basic working knowledge of how to handle polarity in the context of religious worship can be quite adequate by itself.

It's fascinating to see how many aspects of traditional congregational worship, and the cultural forms that surround it, make sense when understood from the point of view of polarity. Since ancient times, for example, Christian priests and ministers have nearly always been men, and the core members of the congregation have usually been women—church ladies, not church gentlemen, are the social and devotional heart of most Christian churches. This makes it easier for the etheric currents to flow: most women have masculine etheric bodies and most men have feminine etheric bodies, so the most influential people in the congregation are likely to have subtle bodies adapted to send an ample supply of life force and the celebrant is just as likely to have a subtle body adapted to receive it.

Readers of nineteenth- and early twentieth-century literature will also be aware that unmarried and widowed women active in church congregations are legendary for cultivating erotic fantasies about their ministers. "Old maid's insanity," the delusion on the part of a sexually frustrated woman that a man she admires is secretly in love with her, has been a common hazard faced by parish clergy for centuries. Delusions of this kind are pathological expressions of normal flow of polarity between the celebrant and his female congregants: the same kind of polarity relationship that Adolf Hitler exploited using the ladies of the "varicose veins brigade." It is not at all impossible, in fact, that one of the reasons that Christian churches have put such a premium on female celibacy is that this provides so robust a source of energy for church services to work with.

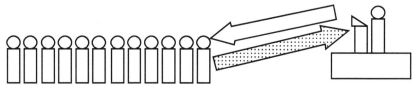

When religious services are badly handled, the minister gathers up the etheric force from the congregation but does not transmit it, and so no astral current descends. Secondhand methods of stirring up emotion are typically used in such services to imitate the astral effect.

An ineffective religious service

That source of power becomes a source of serious problems once the celebrant no longer maintains a working relationship with the deity he is supposed to worship, or simply has no idea how to offer up the etheric energy from the congregation to that deity, as a result of clumsy modernizations of the liturgy and the clergy training process. Once that happens, the celebrant stops being a middleman and becomes the repository of all the excess etheric energy in the congregation, while being expected to provide astral energy to the entire congregation. If the celebrant has no particular talent for public speaking or entertainment, and cannot meet the astral needs of the congregation, the church slides into the first kind of dysfunction described above. The polarity relationship between celebrant and congregation breaks down, the congregation stops sending an etheric current to the minister, and everything settles into the kind of dull routine that American Christians know all too well.

On the other hand, if the celebrant is a charismatic performer, or if he or she makes use of artificial tricks such as pop-music worship bands and theatrical devices to stir up the emotions of the congregation, the second mode of failure follows promptly. Every Sunday, the celebrant receives a robust helping of etheric energy from the congregation, and unless he knows what to do with this—and few clergypeople have this kind of training nowadays—it naturally seeks release in the time-honored fashion. Since an outflow of etheric energy in sexual encounters is more typically feminine than masculine, furthermore, clergymen in this situation who had no previous orientation toward gay sex quite often find themselves attracted to male lovers, who can draw out the excess etheric force.

Equally, and far more destructively, they may begin preying on children. Before the age of puberty, as noted earlier, children have etheric bodies adapted to absorb etheric energy from adults in nonsexual contact. This can tempt the corrupted minister to offload excess etheric energy into them through sexual molestation, with disastrous results.

Meanwhile the congregation's constant demand for astral energy very often drives clergy in this situation to alcohol, which artificially stimulates the astral body. The result is the classic type of the failed clergyman, alcoholic, sexually unfaithful, morally depraved, and subject to rounds of the kind of serious depression that can inspire any number of bad decisions. This result is all too common nowadays, and it is almost entirely avoidable given adequate knowledge and training. Yet an important factor needs to be understood to make mass polarity workings function and avoid these and other problems: the nature of the collective consciousness formed in mass polarity workings.

The nature of the groupmind

It is not accidental that each of the examples that began this chapter used familiar structures: musical performances, church services, and political rallies. Most people in the Western world have been to all three of these at least a few times, and nearly everybody has at least a basic grasp of what is happening, what the important events mean, and what they will be expected to do. That familiarity is an important ally in mass polarity workings, because a certain amount of comfort on the part of the audience is essential in order to accomplish the most important step in these workings: the formation of a groupmind.

A groupmind is a temporary collective consciousness formed any time a group of people share a single focus of attention and a common emotional state. Rock concerts, church services, and political rallies all depend for part of their collective effect on the formation of a group-mind, whether or not polarity magic is involved. So do many other common social events such as sports games. Familiarity, passivity, and shared emotion: these are the features that make a groupmind form and function.

Thus one convenient way to see a groupmind in action is to watch people gathered around a television to watch a sports program. Sometimes gradually, sometimes as fast as though someone flipped a switch, the mood shifts and all attention flows toward what is happening on the screen. Unrelated conversations fall silent, inhibitions break down, and before long the people watching the game are cheering or groaning in unison, caught up in a consciousness simpler and stronger than their ordinary minds. The groupmind only lasts until the game is over, but the people who participate in it will usually find it easier to enter into a similar groupmind in the future. For many people, in fact, participation in a groupmind can be addictive—again, sports fandom is a good place to see this in action.

All these features make a groupmind as problematic as it is power-ful, for groupminds are by definition less intelligent, less reasonable, and less restrained than the individual minds that flow together to cre-ate them. The reason for this is rooted in the planes of being discussed in Chapters 3 and 4. Individual human minds function mostly on the astral plane, the plane of imagination and emotion, but they are influ-enced to at least some degree by the next plane up—the mental plane, the plane of meanings, purposes, and values. Groupminds, by contrast, are purely astral phenomena. They occupy the same place on the ladder of being as the minds of animals, and not necessarily the more intelli-gent animals, either.

This is why mobs of people caught up in collective emotion can com-mit cruelties that no member of the mob would think of doing as an individual. It is also why soldiers in battle, caught up in the groupmind of their platoon or company, will sometimes try things that no sane per-son would attempt, and sometimes fall into a blind panic completely out of their individual character and flee from the enemy they have pledged to fight. Groupminds are powerful and they are also danger-ous, and this leads to the first requirement of a successful mass polar-ity working: *the mage who is guiding the working must remain outside the groupmind.*

Most of the arrangements of church services, political rallies, and other gatherings where mass polarity functions are designed to help maintain that separation. This is why the celebrants in church services are separated from the congregation by various material and symbolic barriers, for example. The change in floor level between the area where the congregation sits and the area where the celebrant stands is one of the most common of these.

Yet it's far from rare for people who are leading religious services, political rallies, and the like to be caught up in the same groupmind they have helped generate in the rest of the participants, and sink to the same level of consciousness. At best, this causes the working to dissolve into the same kind of rush of libido that makes a rock concert what it is. At worst, it can swamp the conscious mind completely and lead the mage and his followers alike to believe absurdities, act on them, and fall victim to them. The self-destruction of the Third Reich under Adolf Hitler is a fine example. Having convinced his followers that he was invincible, Hitler was absorbed by their groupmind, came to believe this himself, and led his nation straight into a suicidal two-front war against both of the world's two largest industrial and military powers. *Götterdämmerung* followed promptly.

It takes a fair degree of mental focus and self-mastery to hold onto individual consciousness in such situations. Succeed at this difficult task, however, and it becomes possible to relate to the groupmind of the audience as though it was a single person. That allows polarity work to be done with the full power of the groupmind on one side, and whatever resources the mage can bring to the interaction on the other. Add in the presence of a deity, invoked through personal devotion or ritual means, and a three-pole working of the kind discussed earlier in this chapter becomes a powerful mode of polarity magic.

The Guild of the Master Jesus

Here again Dion Fortune's work offers a useful example. One of the subsidiary groups of her Fraternity of the Inner Light, as mentioned earlier, was a congregational religious body called the Guild of the Master Jesus. Its rituals and instructional documents have only just been made public, but copies were put in circulation in the American occult community by longtime occultist Carr P. Collins many years ago, and I have had the chance to study them. The recent publication of the

Guild's papers is a great advantage to students of polarity magic and the esoteric side of Christian spirituality.[32]

Members of the Guild went through a training program that focused on prayer and meditation, with Fortune's volume of Christian theological reflections, *Mystical Meditations on the Collects* (1930), as the principal textbook. The methods of meditation taught to members in the three preliminary degrees focused on building up forms in the imagination, and the forms used were taken from familiar Bible passages. Students in meditation thus imagined themselves being present when this or that incident from the Old or New Testament took place, and made the imagined scene as vivid and realistic as possible.

Each initiate of the higher levels of the Guild also had a shrine at home that featured the distinctive emblem of the Guild, which centered on a Celtic cross, along with flowers, a burning lamp, and incense. At this home shrine the initiate practiced daily prayers and meditations. The central activity of the Guild, however, was a form of the standard Christian communion ritual, and this was where polarity entered into the Guild's system.

Unlike most versions of the Christian communion ceremony, the Guild's ritual of the Celebration of the Holy Communion required two clergypersons, one male and the other female. The clergyman had the title of Ministrant, and he sat to the north of the altar, on the left from the perspective of the congregation. The clergywoman had the title of Lector, and she sat to the south of the altar, on the right as the congregation faced them. The two were of equal importance and authority, but they had different roles in the outward forms of the ritual—and also in its inward, magical and spiritual dimension. As the Guild papers explain, "The Ministrant works with the invisible forces and builds forms to channel their manifestation. The Lector works with the group-mind of the congregation."

In terms of the analysis given earlier in this chapter, the two celebrants divided up the polarity work of the service. The Lector established and maintained the flow of polarity with the congregation, while the Ministrant established and maintained the flow of polarity with Christ. The natural polarity between the two celebrants made it easy for etheric energy to flow from the Lector to the Ministrant and astral energy from the Ministrant to the Lector, completing the circuit. The division of labor between two celebrants also decreased the risk of the problems mentioned earlier in this chapter.

---

[32] Fortune and Gilson 2024.

It is interesting to note that this same pattern of having a male and a female clergyperson up in front of the congregation has also been adopted in many American Protestant churches, most of whose members have never heard of Dion Fortune. The reason here is simple enough. In modern American Protestantism, women no longer have the dominant role in church they once did, and it has therefore become necessary to set up a polarity relationship that draws on the force provided by physically male (and thus etherically female) members of the congregation. This makes the flow of polarity more complex, but it also makes it more balanced: there is less risk of etheric overload on the part of the celebrant, since the female celebrant can let excess etheric energy flow back to male congregants, and also less risk of astral exhaustion, since the inflow of astral force from male congregants can help make up any deficit.

The congregation thus inevitably plays a less passive role in this form of work than in the standard church ceremony. The training provided by the Guild to its ordinary members was as important as the more advanced training given to the Ministrants and Lectors. As the Guild papers indicate, "This training aims at producing lay workers who will be able to assist the priests in their work of teaching." In private rituals of the Guild, these lay workers were supplemented by four advanced initiates, two men and two women, who sat in the sanctuary of the church near the altar and provided a further dimension of assistance.

That assistance was magical in nature, because the work of the celebrant or celebrants in any mass polarity working is made much easier when at least a few members of the congregation understand the inner side of the work and can cooperate intelligently with it. Even if most of the congregation has no idea what is going on, the leaven provided by the handful of instructed members assists considerably in keeping the energy moving and empowering the work the celebrants have to do. All these practices worked to decrease the magical burden placed on an individual celebrant in mass polarity workings—and all of them can be adapted for use in other forms of mass polarity working.

The Rites of Isis and Pan

The structure of polarity flows used by the Guild of the Master Jesus, as already noted, was the standard approach to Christian congregational worship, and is also found in many other religious traditions in the modern world, especially in the West. It is not, however, the only option. Two thousand years ago a radically different structure was more common in the Western world. In those days religious ceremonies focused on life, strength, and fertility rather than the spiritual uplifting of the congregation, and the polarity workings that were part of those rites reversed the flows of the modern method.

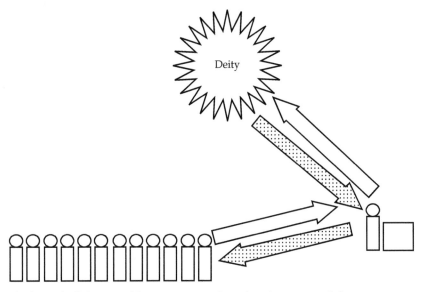

The form of religious worship more common in ancient times reversed the flows, so that what worshippers gained from the deity was life and strength channeled through the etheric plane. Dion Fortune worked with this same pattern in her Rites of Isis and Pan.

Ancient religious rites

The ancient approach, like the modern one, has three roles: the congregation, the celebrant, and the deity. In ancient rites, however, the congregation was primarily male, and provided astral force to the celebrant, who passed it onto the deity. The deity responded with a return current of etheric force, which passed through the celebrant to strengthen and vitalize the congregation. In an age when the fertility of fields, flocks, and human beings was a central concern, this was a compelling and valued approach to worship.

Some of the core differences between ancient and modern Western religious traditions can be understood as adaptations to this change in energy flows. In ancient religious rites it was not merely standard practice but an act of religious reverence to provide worshippers with vivid images of the gods and goddesses they invoked. Ancient Greek temples were thus adorned with huge statues of their deities fashioned from gold and ivory, imported at great expense and crafted by the finest artists in the country. This provided a potent support to the imaginations of the worshippers and thus strengthened their capacity to contribute astral energy to the work. Many more recent religious traditions, by contrast, refuse to portray their deities in pictorial form, or do so only in very restricted ways, to prevent the reverse flow of astral energy.

Similarly, celibacy was not valued in ancient religious rites, except in very specific contexts where etheric force was needed. Nor was sexual imagery considered out of place in a religious context. Ancient Greek religious processions routinely carried giant wooden penises as emblems of the overflowing fertility and vitality of the deities the Greeks worshipped. Here again, concrete images were being used to stir the imagination, but there is another aspect to imagery of this kind, and to the more robust forms of sexual practice that some faiths included in their worship. No one was expected to offer up their own etheric energy to the deity; instead, the deity provided the gift of life force, while the worshippers offered astral energy in return.

Finally, the place of animal sacrifice in ancient Western religion needs to be understood in this context. Before the invention of the refrigerator, the only way to keep meat fresh was to keep it on the hoof, and it was therefore an everyday task to kill meat animals before a meal. Animal sacrifices in ancient times were in effect community barbecues in which a god or goddess was the guest of honor, and meat was provided in what was then the normal way. At the same time, the act of killing an animal releases a jolt of etheric force, and this was used to "prime the pump" and get the etheric current flowing.

We live in a different age with different standards. Fortunately animal sacrifice is by no means the only way to set etheric forces moving. Here, too, Dion Fortune and her Fraternity of the Inner Light were pioneers. The Rites of Isis and Pan, written by Fortune and performed for selected audiences by members of her Fraternity, are among other things elegant examples of the ancient style of polarity work.

Both rituals are enacted principally by a priest and a priestess, just as in the Guild of the Master Jesus, but their roles are not quite so straightforwardly divided as in that latter rite. The priest in both rites leads the audience in formulating the temple and works with the energies of the audience, taking on the role the female participant fills in the Guild ceremony. The invocation of the deity, however, is performed by the priestess when Pan is to be invoked, and the priest when Isis descends, using the sexual polarity between the celebrants to empower the working.

In both rituals, in the climactic moments of the working, one of the celebrants becomes the vessel for the invoked deity: the priest takes on the godform and speaks in the name of Pan, and the priestess takes on the godform and speaks in the name of Isis. In each case it is the participant who has taken on the godform who becomes the intermediary between the deity and the audience, sending out etheric blessings of life and health to all who take part in the working.

Because there are celebrants of both sexes, however, each member of the audience is also likely to polarize with whichever of the celebrants suits his or her orientation. As a result, a great deal of astral and etheric energy moves back and forth during the working. Considerable skill is needed to handle the various forces effectively, and it is very often useful in workings of this kind to have a small group of experienced mages present who sit on the sidelines and do nothing but work with the currents of force.

The Rites of Pan and Isis are well worth close study, and fortunately they have been published in full.[33] They can be performed exactly as written, but they also make useful templates on which a great many other rituals can be based. Since the older style of ritual is not well documented in its ancient Western forms, mages interested in working with this style of mass polarity magic can learn a great deal from these examples.

Designing a mass polarity working

As the points raised above may suggest, there are at least two ways to craft an effective mass polarity working. The most common approach is to start with an existing ritual and add polarity to it. If you intend to explore mass polarity workings, this is a good place to start, whether or not your working will be open to the general public. Many kinds of ritual can be worked in this way, from congregational worship to lodge initiation and beyond. So long as the ritual you have in mind

---

[33] Knight 2013.

has room for a group of people who can take on the role of audience or congregation, and also has a place for one or two people who become the focus of attention during the working, it should be possible to empower it with mass polarity work.

The more difficult approach is to come up with an original ritual that will function as a focus for mass polarity. This is considerably more complex, since it takes skill and practice to draft a ritual structure and language that will attract and hold the attention, emotions, and etheric forces of an audience. The Rites of Isis and Pan demonstrate that this can be done effectively; those readers who have witnessed any significant amount of public ritual in recent years will know from personal experience that it can also be done very, very badly! If you choose this approach, study as many successful examples as you can, and be willing to accept advice from the other people you work with.

Another issue that must be faced early on is the choice of a deity to invoke. The custom of invoking a deity for the third participant in workings of this kind is not simply a matter of habit. On the one hand, the third pole in such a working needs to be filled by a being with whom the mage or mages at the center of the working can direct adoration and affection, so that the energy channels can be established and the two-way flow of energies set in motion. On the other, as Aleister Crowley liked to point out, whether gods and the like exist or not, the universe certainly seems to behave as though they do.

The choice of a deity to work with in this way will in many cases be predetermined by the nature of the ritual being worked. In others, it will depend on the personal devotions and practices of the mage or mages who will be conducting the work. In some cases, however, it is possible for the human participants in the project to choose from among several deities. This choice should be made with considerable care, and the deity in question should be consulted by way of divination or whatever other method is suitable.

Adolf Hitler's case is again worth noting. While he was careful not to reveal any of the details of the magical workings he performed, a perceptive 1936 essay by psychologist Carl Jung noted that a great many signs suggested a connection between Hitler and the ancient Germanic god Wotan.[34] Jung knew a great deal about occultism—his doctoral dissertation was on the psychological dimensions of occult

---

[34] Jung 1964.

phenomena—and he also had extensive contacts throughout the Central European occult scene, so his testimony should be taken seriously.

If Hitler was invoking Wotan in his mass polarity workings, that would explain a great many things, including the way that Nazi Germany proceeded through a series of startling political and military successes to total failure and defeat. If you invoke a deity with enough force, you can expect to share at least some dimensions of his fate, and the myths of Wotan all lead straight to the downfall of the gods.

Beyond the choice of a ritual, the choice of a deity, and the various measures that can be used to create a groupmind, the practice of mass polarity workings must be left to the individual practitioner and the group he or she works with. This is a powerful, effective, and potentially very dangerous mode of working. Those who take part in it need to be aware of the risks they run, and should be sure they have adequate training and preparation before they begin—for example, ample experience with the less demanding workings in this book.

There is, however, another good reason to be familiar with mass polarity workings. As I mentioned at the beginning of this chapter, mass polarity workings are tolerably common these days, and many of the people who are involved in them have no idea that magic is being practiced on them. Becoming aware of the structure of mass polarity workings can make it easier to avoid being caught up unawares in magical workings of this kind, and can provide ways of escaping from their influence. Here as so often in magic, a word to the wise is sufficient.

RESOURCES

Ashcroft-Nowicki, Dolores (1991). *The Tree of Ecstasy.* London: Aquarian.

Atkinson, William Walker (1909). *The Mystery of Sex or Sex Polarity.* Chicago, IL: Arcane Book Concern.

Atkinson, William Walker (as "Three Initiates") (1913). *The Kybalion.* Chicago, IL: Yogi Publication Society.

Avalon, Arthur (1950). *The Serpent Power.* Madras: Ganesh & Co.

Berg, Wendy, and Mike Harris (2003). *Polarity Magic.* Woodfield, MN: Llewellyn.

Bertiaux, Michael (1988). *The Vodoun Gnostic Workbook.* New York: Magickal Childe.

Billington, Penny, and Ian Rees (2022). *The Keys to the Temple.* London: Aeon Books.

Blavatsky, Helena Petrovna (1889). *Esoteric Section Instructions.* London: privately printed.

Corbin, Henry (1976). *Mundus Imaginalis, or the Imaginary and the Imaginal.* Ipswich, UK: Golgonooza Press.

Culianu, Ioan P. (1987). *Eros and Magic in the Renaissance.* Chicago, IL: The University of Chicago Press.

Davies, Ann (n.d.). *Qabalistic Doctrines on Sexual Polarity.* Los Angeles, CA: Builders of the Adytum.

Deveney, John Patrick (1997). *Paschal Beverly Randolph: A Nineteenth-Century Black American Spiritualist, Rosicrucian, and Sex Magician*. Albany, NY: SUNY Press.

Doczi, György (1981). *The Power of Limits: Proportional Harmonies in Nature, Art, and Architecture*. Boston, MA: Shambhala.

Douglas, Nik, and Penny Slinger (2000). *Sexual Secrets: The Alchemy of Ecstasy*. Rochester, VT: Destiny.

Fielding, Charles, and Carr P. Collins (1998). *The Story of Dion Fortune*. Loughborough, UK: Thoth.

Fortune, Dion (1930). *Mystical Meditations on the Collects*. London: Rider.

Fortune, Dion (1966). *The Cosmic Doctrine*. Cheltenham, UK: Helios Book Service.

Fortune, Dion (1978). *Moon Magic*. York Beach, ME: Weiser.

Fortune, Dion (1978). *The Sea Priestess*. York Beach, ME: Weiser.

Fortune, Dion (1980). *The Goat Foot God*. York Beach, ME: Weiser.

Fortune, Dion (1980). *The Winged Bull*. York Beach, ME: Weiser.

Fortune, Dion (1988). *The Esoteric Philosophy of Love and Marriage and The Problem of Purity*. Wellingborough, UK: Aquarian.

Fortune, Dion (2000). *The Cosmic Doctrine*, Millennium Edition. York Beach, ME: Weiser.

Fortune, Dion (n.d.). *Guild of the Master Jesus papers*. (unpublished)

Fortune, Dion, and Gareth Knight (1998). *The Circuit of Force*. Loughborough, UK: Thoth.

Fortune, Dion, and Christian Gilson (2024). A Path to the Grail. London: Holythorn Press.

Giebel, Rolf W., trans. (2009). *The Mahavairocanabhisambhodhi Sutra*. Berkeley, CA: Numata Center for Buddhist Translation and Research.

Ginzburg, Carlo (1991). *Ecstasies: Deciphering the Witch's Sabbath*. New York: Pantheon.

Gould, A., and Franklin L. Dubois (1911). *The Science of Sex Regeneration*. Chicago, IL: Advanced Thought Publishing.

Grant, Kenneth (1992). *Hecate's Fountain*. London: Skoob Books.

Grant, Kenneth (1994). *Outer Gateways*. London: Skoob Books.

Greer, John Michael (2017). *Circles of Power*. London: Aeon Books.

Greer, John Michael (2020). *The Dolmen Arch* (2 volumes). Portland, OR: Azoth Press.

Greer, John Michael (2023). *A Commentary on The Cosmic Doctrine*. London: Aeon Books. (Cited as Greer 2023a.)

Greer, John Michael (2023). *Modern Order of Essenes Apprentice Manual*. East Providence, RI: published online. (Cited as Greer 2023b.)

Greer, John Michael (2023). *The Secret of the Five Rites*. London: Aeon Books. (Cited as Greer 2023c.)

Jung, C.G. (1964). "Wotan." In Jung, C.G., *Civilization in Transition*, trans. R.F.C Hull. Princeton, NJ: Princeton University Press, pp. 371–399.

King, Francis (1970). *The Rites of Modern Occult Magic*. New York: Macmillan.

King, Francis (1971). *Sexuality, Magic, and Perversion*. Secaucus, NJ: Citadel.

King, Francis (1973). *The Secret Rituals of the O.T.O.* London: C.W. Daniels.

Kiyota, Minoru (1977). *Shingon Buddhism: Theory and Practice*. Los Angeles, CA: Buddhist Books International.

Knight, Gareth, ed. (2013). *Dion Fortune's Rites of Isis and of Pan*. Cheltenham, UK: Skylight.

Lévi, Eliphas (2017). *The Doctrine and Ritual of High Magic*, trans. John Michael Greer and Mark Mikituk. New York: Tarcher Perigee.

Lipp, Deborah (2023). *Bending the Binary*. Woodfield, MN: Llewellyn.

Long, Max Freedom (1946). "The Thrice-Coiled Serpent," in *The Flying Roll* 2 (1946), pp. 36–41.

Mead, G.R.S. (1919). *The Doctrine of the Subtle Body in Western Tradition*. London: Watkins.

Miles, Austin (1989). *Don't Call Me Brother*. Buffalo, NY: Prometheus.

Montfaucon de Villars, N. de, Abbé (1914). *Le Comte de Gabalis*, trans. Lotus (i.e., Sarah Emery) Dudley. New York: The Brothers.

Motoyama, Hiroshi (1981). *Theories of the Chakras: Bridge to Higher Consciousness*. Wheaton, IL: Theosophical Publishing House.

Nagel, Alexandra (2007). "Marriage with Elementals: From *Le Comte de Gabalis* to a Golden Dawn Ritual." M.A. thesis, University of Amsterdam.

Plato (1961). *Symposium*, trans. Michael Joyce. In Hamilton, Edith, and Huntington Cairns, eds., *The Collected Dialogues of Plato*. Princeton, NJ: Princeton University Press.

Plummer, George Winslow (1923). *Rosicrucian Manual*. New York: Mercury.

Powell, Arthur A. (1925). *The Etheric Double*. Wheaton, IL: Theosophical Publishing House.

Powell, Arthur A. (1927). *The Astral Body*. Wheaton, IL: Theosophical Publishing House.

Powell, Arthur A. (1927). *The Mental Body*. Wheaton, IL: Theosophical Publishing House.

Randolph, Paschal Beverly (1873). *The Ansairetic Mystery*. Toledo, OH: Liberal Printing House.

Randolph, Paschal Beverly (1874). *Eulis! The History of Love*. Toledo, OH: Randolph Publishing Co.

Reeder, David H. (1916). *Private Sex Lessons*. Chicago, IL: Advanced Thought Publishing.

Regardie, Israel (1945). *The Middle Pillar*. Chicago, IL: Aries.

Regardie, Israel (2015). *The Golden Dawn*. Woodbury, MN: Llewellyn.

Richardson, Alan (1985). *Dancers to the Gods*. Wellingborough, UK: Aquarian.

Richardson, Alan (2007). *Priestess: The Life and Magic of Dion Fortune.* Loughborough, UK: Thoth.

Richardson, Alan, and Geoff Hughes (1992). *Ancient Magicks for a New Age.* St. Paul, MN: Llewellyn.

Robson, Vivian (1937). *Electional Astrology.* Philadelphia, PA: Lippincott.

Schmidt, Leigh Eric (2010). *Heaven's Bride.* New York: Basic Books.

Schneider, Herbert W., and George Lawton (1942). *A Prophet and a Pilgrim: Being the Incredible History of Thomas Lake Harris and Laurence Oliphant.* New York: Columbia University Press.

Selby, John (2008). "Dion Fortune and her Inner Plane Contacts: Intermediaries in the Western Esoteric Tradition." Ph.D. dissertation, University of Exeter.

Urban, Hugh B. (2006). *Magia Sexualis: Sex, Magic, and Liberation in Modern Western Esotericism.* Berkeley, CA: University of California Press.

van Raalte, Georgia (2015). "Tea, Scones, and Socially Responsible Sex Magic: The Egalitarian Occultism of Dion Fortune." M.A. thesis, University of Amsterdam.

Waite, Arthur Edward (1960). *The Holy Kabbalah.* New Hyde Park, NY: University Books.

Warnock, Christopher (2010). *Secrets of Planetary Magic.* Iowa City, IA: Renaissance Astrology.

Williams, Charles (1941). *Witchcraft.* London: Faber and Faber.

Yamasaki, Taikō (1988). *Shingon: Japanese Esoteric Buddhism,* trans. Richard and Cynthia Peterson. Boston, MA: Shambhala.

INDEX